A CHALLENGE!

Whitney's eyes narrowed. "I bet that vicious horse goes completely crazy out here," she taunted. "Has he tried to kill you yet?"

Kerry's blood was starting to boil. In spite of her determination not to let Whitney's goading get to her, she could feel her temper rising. She took a deep breath. "I'll match Buccaneer against your horse any day."

Whitney smiled. This was just what she'd been hoping for—a direct challenge that she was sure to win. "What's wrong with right now?"

"Out *here*?" Kerry replied in surprise.

"I'll race you on the cross-country course. And *beat* you," Whitney declared, ignoring Robin's protest. "What's the matter, Kerry? Scared of being beaten . . . again?"

BEST FRIENDS

JUMPING INTO TROUBLE

BY MAGGIE DANA

ILLUSTRATIONS BY DONNA RUFF

Troll Associates

To Jane Stine

Library of Congress Cataloging in Publication Data

Dana, Maggie.
  Jumping into trouble.

  (Best Friends; #2)
  Summary: Kerry enjoys her job as live-in companion
to a handicapped girl and helper at a horse stables
until a jealous neighbor tries to force her out of
her position.
  [1. Horses—Fiction. 2. Friendship—Fiction.
3. Physically handicapped—Fiction] I. Ruff, Donna,
ill. II. Title. III. Series: Best friends
(Mahwah, N.J.)
PZ7.D194Ju 1988   [Fic]   87-16248
ISBN 0-8167-1193-3 (lib. bdg.)
ISBN 0-8167-1194-1 (pbk.)

A TROLL BOOK, published by Troll Associates,
Mahwah, NJ 07430

BEST FRIENDS

JUMPING INTO TROUBLE

Chapter One

The large moving van was the first thing Kerry Logan saw as she came out of the woods that bordered Timber Ridge Stables. The van took up most of the Blakes' driveway, and two men were carrying an enormous white sofa up the loading ramp. "Hey, Holly, isn't that Monica's house?"

Holly Chapman skidded her wheelchair to a stop, sending a small shower of gravel out behind her. "Yes," she said. "I wonder what's up." And then she laughed. "If Monica Blake's moving, Whitney won't have a friend in the world."

Kerry shuddered. Whitney Myers was the only bad part about living at Timber Ridge. Ever since she'd arrived in Vermont at the beginning of the summer, Whitney had made a career out of making Kerry's life as miserable as possible.

"Maybe your mother knows something about it," Kerry said, pushing a stray lock of hair off her forehead. She was hot and sticky, and her dark brown hair was plastered to her head. "Hey, we'd better hurry up. She wants us back by five."

As they approached the stables' driveway, Kerry glanced up toward Timber Ridge Mountain and caught her breath. It wasn't the highest mountain in Vermont, but it had some of the steepest ski trails in the state.

Kerry paused for a moment, admiring the majestic beauty of the mountain. She'd always wanted to ski, but had never had the chance. There weren't any mountains near her home in Connecticut. As images of brightly dressed skiers filtered through her mind, Kerry wondered if she'd still be at Timber Ridge when winter arrived. When she'd taken the job as live-in companion to Holly, Liz Chapman had told her that she would only be needed until school started in September. But Kerry had to stay in Vermont until her father returned from the Middle East. If he wasn't back by the fall, Kerry guessed she'd have to go and live with her aunt Molly, who had an apartment in the village, until he returned.

Pulling her scattered thoughts together, Kerry smiled and waved as Liz Chapman came out of the indoor riding arena and ran toward them. Liz, with her short, blond hair and deep blue eyes so much like Holly's, looked young enough to be Holly's sister instead of her mother.

"Phew, I'm glad you're back," Liz said. "I've got everything ready for you, Kerry. Just put the feed in the horses' mangers, and don't forget to check their water buckets. They've already had their hay." She stopped, almost out of breath. "Have I forgotten anything?"

Holly grinned, her deep blue eyes sparkling with fun. "You haven't told us where you're going."

"Oh," her mother said absent-mindedly. "Sorry about that. I'll be home tonight around nine or so."

"Mom," Holly said, "don't you *want* to tell us?"

Kerry winked at her. "Maybe she has a date, and she doesn't want to tell us about it."

"A date?" Liz asked, sounding puzzled. "Who's got a date?"

"Come on, Mom," Holly said between giggles. "It's okay if you've got some secret admirer and you're too embarrassed to let on. It's okay. I understand."

"Holly, I haven't got a clue what you're talking about, and I don't have time to find out. I'm already late. Look, I'll see you kids later on, okay?"

"Fine, but *where* will you be if we need you for something?" Holly insisted.

"I'll be at Larchwood, checking on a new horse," Liz said.

"You're buying a horse?" Kerry exclaimed. That *was* exciting news. The only horse that the Chapmans owned was Magician, Holly's horse. All the others were either owned by the residents of the wealthy Timber Ridge community, or else they were school horses that belonged to the riding stables.

"Not for me," Liz replied. "It's for Mr. Ballantine, and he's waiting for me now. Look, I promise I'll tell you all about it when I get back. Just make sure the horses don't starve, and check the refrigerator if you two get hungry." She glanced at her watch again.

3

"Mrs. Myers will be furious if I keep him waiting."

"Who? Your mysterious date?" Holly teased.

"No. Mr. Ballantine." Liz shot her daughter an exasperated look. "I really don't have time to explain now," she said, and started toward her car. Moments later they heard her rev the engine loudly and back out of the driveway much faster than usual.

"Boy, she was sure in a hurry, wasn't she?" Kerry said with a smile. "I wonder what's got her all steamed up?"

"I don't know," Holly murmured, "but whoever Mr. Ballantine is, he must be something really special. Mom hasn't dated anyone since my father died."

"Mmmm," Kerry said thoughtfully. "I wonder what she meant when she said Mrs. Myers would be furious if she kept Mr. Ballantine waiting."

Holly dissolved into a fit of laughter. "I wonder if the old witch has set her up on a blind date."

Kerry started to giggle. They didn't like Mrs. Myers any better than her spoiled brat of a daughter. It was no wonder Whitney was such a creep, with a mother like Mrs. Myers. The bossy, overbearing woman was president of the Timber Ridge Homeowners' Association, and she was forever interfering with Liz's efforts to run the riding stables.

The horses all began neighing at once as they heard Kerry and Holly open the barn doors. "I'll hand you the buckets," Holly said, and wheeled herself into the feed room.

Kerry quickly entered each horse's stall and dispensed grain to the hungry occupant. In Magician's stall she lingered a little longer, admiring the big black

4

horse as he eagerly stuck his nose into the manger. He was her favorite of all the horses, and riding him, she'd helped the Timber Ridge riding team win the Hampshire Classic Challenge Cup. Although he belonged to Holly, Holly hadn't been on him since the accident that left her legs paralyzed. Kerry wondered if her friend would ever ride her horse again.

"You know," Kerry said when they'd finished feeding the horses, "we forgot to ask your mother if she knows who's moving into the Blakes' house."

"No problem," Holly muttered under her breath as the door opened and a slim, fashionably dressed girl entered the barn. "Whitney's here. Her mother's the biggest gossip at Timber Ridge. She'll know who it is."

Whitney Myers picked her way daintily toward them, her nose wrinkling in disgust as she tried to avoid stepping in the stray piles of dirty bedding and manure that still littered the floor. Wearing white slacks, a pale blue silk shirt that matched her eyes, and white ankle-strap sandals, she didn't look as if she'd come to help out with the barn chores. Her long dark hair was piled on top of her head, held in place with two tortoiseshell combs, making her look much older than fifteen.

"Has anyone seen my radio?" she asked in a cool voice. "I left it here this morning."

"Mom put it in the tackroom," Holly replied. "But you'd better not bring it to the barn again."

"Why?"

"Because it's a fire hazard, Whitney. The plug's broken."

"Oh, yeah, says who?" Whitney snapped. "What makes you the expert, Holly? I didn't know you were an electrician."

Holly held her temper. "My mother said not to bring it back again until it's fixed, okay?"

Whitney frowned. She hated people telling her what to do. Flashing an angry look at both of them, she turned and headed for the tackroom.

"Hey, Whitney!" Holly called out. "We just saw a moving van down the road, at Monica's house. Are the Blakes moving out?"

Whitney stopped and turned around. "Yes, they are," she said sarcastically. "Is that okay with you?"

Holly ignored the jibe. "Gee," she said innocently, "what a shame. I guess you've just lost your best friend, huh?"

Kerry bit her lip to keep from smiling. What Holly said was true. Without Monica Blake in the picture, Whitney would have no one to boss around.

Whitney shrugged. "Big deal," she said nonchalantly. "Monica was getting to be a drag anyway. Now, if you'll stop bothering me, I'm going to get my radio and go home."

"Aren't you going to tell us who's moving in?" Holly insisted. "Surely *you* know who it is."

Whitney's eyes narrowed. "Give me one good reason why I ought to tell you."

"Because you know who it is, and I bet you're just dying to tell someone," Holly said.

"Never mind, Holly," Kerry interrupted. Trying to get information out of Whitney was hopeless. "Let's go back to the house. We'll ask Liz when she gets back."

"Oh, she's gone, then?" Whitney said. "Good. My mother was afraid she'd be late. Mr. Ballantine hates to be kept waiting."

Holly forgot all about the new family; Whitney's remark had just reminded her of this afternoon's other unsolved mystery. She tried to sound casual. "Who's Mr. Ballantine, Whitney?"

"You're full of questions today, aren't you?" Whitney drawled slowly as she flicked a piece of hay off her white pants. "Which one shall I answer first?"

Holly's face slipped into a scowl, but Kerry nudged her quickly. They'd never get any information out of Whitney if they aggravated her.

"Liz told us she was going to Larchwood to look at a horse, and that she was meeting a Mr. Ballantine," Kerry said as calmly as she could. "We thought you might know who he was."

"He's an old friend of my father's," Whitney replied in a haughty tone. "He's buying one of Larchwood's best horses, and my mother told Liz to go and check it out for him. He's sending it here for a couple of months, and *I'm* going to ride it for him."

"Does he live at Timber Ridge?" Kerry asked, trying to picture which of the elegant homes might belong to him.

Whitney laughed scornfully. "No, but then you wouldn't know that, would you? *You* only work here."

Kerry flinched, and then felt the pressure of Holly's hand on her arm. She knew what it meant: Don't let Whitney know how much her cutting remark had hurt her. It only made the girl worse.

"Oh, and since you're so interested," Whitney

8

continued, "the new family's name is McKenna. Also old friends of my parents. My mother went to school with Mrs. McKenna, and I can't wait for Jennifer to get here."

"Jennifer?" Holly asked curiously.

"My best friend, Jennifer McKenna," Whitney replied, stressing the word best. "She'll be here this weekend." Whitney paused and stared at Kerry, her eyes glinting dangerously. "Just you wait till you see her ride," she said ominously. "She's a much better rider than you, Kerry Logan. You'll never get on the riding team now."

Holly blew her cool. "Wrong!" she shouted. "Or have you forgotten? Monica Blake's moved out, so Kerry can take *her* place."

Whitney's face held a triumphant smile. "No, you're the one who's wrong, Holly Chapman. The team needs four riders—Robin Lovell, Jennifer McKenna, me, and"—she paused dramatically—"Susan Armstrong."

Kerry gasped. Whitney had gotten the better of them this time. They'd forgotten all about Sue, who was getting over a bout of chicken pox but would soon be back on the team.

"If you're all finished with your dumb questions, I'm going home," Whitney said as she headed toward the tackroom. At the door she hesitated, then turned around slowly. "Just don't forget," she said in an icy tone, "Jennifer McKenna is *my* best friend, so you two had better keep away from her."

"She must be really desperate to have a friend," Holly murmured angrily as Whitney flounced out of

9

the stables, her radio firmly tucked under one arm.

"Yeah," Kerry agreed, and she started to sweep the cement aisle that ran between the two rows of horse stalls. "But who cares? If Jennifer McKenna is Whitney's best friend, she's bound to be just as obnoxious."

Holly laughed. "You're right, but there is one thing that's worrying me."

Kerry swept the last pile of manure into the corner and leaned the broom against the wall. "What?"

"If Jennifer's really a good rider, you know Mrs. Myers will make my mother put her on the team."

"But we've only got Whitney's word for it," Kerry said. "She's probably exaggerating, like she always does."

"Let's hope so," Holly replied. She smiled suddenly. "Hey, now that Monica's gone, Whitney won't have anyone to help her play her nasty little tricks on you!"

Kerry grimaced as she opened the barn door. "Not unless she recruits Jennifer McKenna to do her dirty work for her."

"But why would she? I mean, she got what she wanted. You let her win the individual gold medal at the Hampshire Classic." Holly's smile faded. "You could have beaten her, you know."

Kerry shrugged her shoulders and stood to one side as Holly wheeled herself through the door. But as she followed behind her along the path that led from the stables to the Chapmans' back yard, she couldn't help thinking about what Holly had just said.

It was true. She had let Whitney win the gold medal. But at the time it was the right thing to do.

She had no regrets. Mrs. Myers would never let the Homeowners' Association cancel Liz's contract to run the stables as long as her precious daughter was bringing home gold medals and blue ribbons.

"Let's go for a swim!" Holly cried out as they reached her back yard. "I'm so hot, I think I'm going to melt."

Ten minutes later both girls were in the Chapmans' small, kidney-shaped swimming pool, laughing and splashing each other as they raced toward the deep end, all thoughts of Whitney Myers and the new family forgotten.

As Kerry watched her friend swimming strongly away from her, she thought about Holly's legs. Holly had once been an excellent rider. A car accident, two years ago when she was twelve, had left her paralyzed from the waist down. Liz had confided in her that Holly's doctors really didn't know why she couldn't walk. There was no permanent nerve damage to her spine, and they thought it might even be a psychological handicap—something in Holly's head that prevented her from walking.

"Race you to the other end!" Holly shrieked out, scattering Kerry's thoughts to the wind.

"You're on!" Kerry yelled, but she was no match for her friend. Holly's strong arms and shoulders propelled her through the water swiftly. She was much faster than Kerry, even though Kerry had two perfectly strong legs to help her.

Maybe the doctors were right, Kerry thought as she dived through the water to catch up. Maybe Holly would walk again one day. As she ducked under the

water to avoid the onslaught of Holly's wild splashing, Kerry decided that she couldn't think of anything she wanted more than to see her best friend running around like everyone else—and riding Magician.

Chapter Two

"Hi, Mom. How was your date?" Holly asked when her mother finally returned home at nine o'clock that night, looking pale and tired.

"Huh?" Liz muttered as she kicked off her boots and flopped onto the couch. "What date?"

"Only teasing, Mom. Whitney's already told us about Mr. Ballantine. *And* she also said there's a new family moving in. Do you know anything about them?"

"Not much," Liz answered. "Hey, thanks, Kerry. How did you know I needed a cup of tea?" She smiled gratefully as she took the mug that Kerry had just brought in from the kitchen. "What a night," she said as she sipped the hot tea. "It was a complete waste of my time, and I almost got a speeding ticket on the way there, I was so late."

"Why, Mom?"

"Because I was doing seventy in a fifty-milean-hour zone that's all."

Holly giggled. "Not that, Mom. I meant why was it a waste of your time?"

Liz sighed. "Because Mr. Ballantine had already made up his mind to buy the horse, regardless of what I said."

"I guess you don't like the horse much, huh?"

A slight frown flickered across Liz's face. "He's a good horse, Holly, but . . ." She paused and took another drink of tea. "But he's very high-strung. He'll need a careful, gentle rider, and Mr. Ballantine doesn't strike me as the gentle type."

"Whitney said the horse was coming here for a while," Holly said, "and that she's going to be riding it."

Her mother nodded. "So I hear. Mrs. Myers told me all about it this afternoon." She shook her head slowly. "I wonder when that woman is going to wise up and realize her daughter's not exactly an Olympic rider. This horse will be too much for her. He won't even be easy for *me* to ride."

"Are you driving the van over to pick it up?" Kerry asked.

"No, Larchwood's delivering him tomorrow."

"A new horse *and* Jennifer McKenna," Kerry muttered with a grin. "It's going to be a busy weekend."

Liz yawned and stretched her arms over her head. "I'm ready for bed. I've got a busy day tomorrow. The vet's coming to worm all the horses, and I have to get two new stalls ready."

"Two?" Holly questioned her. "Why two?"

Her mother got to her feet. "Mrs. Myers didn't say

15

an awful lot about the new family, but she did remember to warn me that the daughter had a horse. I figure we'd better be prepared if she's arriving this weekend. Maybe her horse will as well."

"Mom, you haven't said a thing about the new horse from Larchwood," Holly said. "Give us the details."

"His name is Buccaneer, he's about sixteen hands, dark bay, and as temperamental as an opera star. I'm going to have my hands full with this one."

"He doesn't have a wooden leg and a parrot on his shoulder, does he?" Kerry joked as she thought about the horse's name.

Liz laughed. "No, but Mr. Ballantine does look rather like a pirate, now that I think about it. Kind of tall and husky, with bushy eyebrows and a fierce-looking beard."

Holly started to giggle. "Don't tell me he sails around in a boat with a skull and crossbones on it."

"Uh-uh. He's a movie director, and he travels a lot. That's why the horse is coming here. He wants me to work with it while he's away this summer."

With another yawn, Liz disappeared into her bedroom. The moment her door was shut, Holly and Kerry started to speculate on the other new arrival—Jennifer McKenna.

"I wonder what she's like," Kerry said.

"I bet she's awful," Holly replied. "She's got to be if she's already Whitney's best friend." She paused and looked thoughtful for a moment. "You know, it's funny, but Whitney's never talked about her before. I wonder if she's making the whole thing up, about her being a good rider and everything."

Kerry stared at her. "It'd be just like her, wouldn't it? I bet she only said all those things to make me think I'd lose my place on the riding team."

"You're *way* better than the others, so don't worry about it. Mom won't drop you from the team. And besides, we haven't even met Jennifer yet, let alone seen her ride. I bet she's even worse than Whitney."

As Kerry got ready for bed she thought about the newcomer to Timber Ridge. She knew it wasn't really fair to judge a person without knowing her, but she couldn't help feeling that she wasn't going to like Jennifer McKenna one bit.

Buccaneer made a very dramatic arrival at Timber Ridge the next morning. The Larchwood horse van had no sooner pulled into the driveway than he commanded everyone's attention by neighing in alarm and kicking violently at the sides of the van.

"Stand back, kids," Liz ordered as the van's driver lowered the ramp. "I don't trust this animal one bit!"

Kerry pulled Holly's wheelchair to one side while Liz climbed into the front of the van through its small side door. She heard Liz telling the driver to let go of the horse's halter, and in a split second Buccaneer backed violently down the ramp, dragging Liz with him.

Buccaneer's dark bay coat was covered in sweat, and Kerry could see the bright pink membranes that lined his flaring nostrils. The whites of his eyes were showing, and he kept on shaking his head and neighing loudly.

"Easy boy, it's okay," Liz said soothingly as Buccaneer plunged around on the end of his leadrope.

Just then Whitney and a girl with curly brown hair arrived. There was no time for introductions, though. Whitney's eyes lit up when she saw Buccaneer. Pushing rudely past Kerry and Holly, she ran toward the new horse, shrieking with excitement. "He's here, Jennifer!" she yelled loudly.

Buccaneer snorted wildly and reared up, pulling Liz two feet into the air as she struggled to keep hold of him. Kerry almost stopped breathing when it looked as if Liz was going to be caught up in the horse's thrashing front legs.

Liz and Buccaneer battled for control. The horse reared up again, thrashing wildly with his front legs. "Oh, no, you don't!" Liz yelled, and jerked his leadrope sharply. Buccaneer snorted and tried to take a chunk out of her shoulder. Liz danced out of the way just in time. His open mouth missed her by only inches.

Calmly and patiently Liz brought the nervous horse under control, and then turned her attention toward the cause of his crazy behavior. "That was a stupid move, Whitney," she snapped angrily. "I could have been killed. Don't you know any better than to run up to a horse shrieking like a banshee?"

Whitney scowled and then, ignoring Liz, turned toward her new friend. "Come on, Jen. Let's go and see my horse and check out your stall. I bet it hasn't even been cleaned out yet."

Kerry bit her lip, choking back an angry retort. She and Liz had spent the better part of an hour earlier this morning stripping and thoroughly cleaning a

spare stall for Jennifer McKenna's horse.

"What are you going to do with him?" she called out to Liz, who was walking toward the riding ring with the new horse skittering and dancing sideways beside her.

"I'm going to turn him loose for a while and let him settle down," she said. "Open the gate for me, will you?"

As soon as he was free, Buccaneer tore off across the ring, letting off a stream of bone-shattering bucks. He skidded to a stop at the far end, whirled around, and trotted along the rails, his proud head held high, neighing at the top of his lungs.

Kerry leaned over the gate and admired the horse's powerful muscles as they rippled beneath his mahogany-colored coat. He reminded her of a wild stallion, with his long black mane and tail flowing behind him as he raced around.

Holly wheeled herself up and nudged Kerry's ribs. "And Princess Whitney thinks she's going to ride *that*?" she muttered sarcastically.

"I hope he bucks her off," Kerry replied. "What an idiot she is, yelling at the top of her voice like a three-year-old. You'd think she'd never been around a nervous horse before."

Holly grinned. "I wonder what Jennifer thought of her."

"Who knows? But I bet Whitney's madder than a hornet because Liz yelled at her in front of her new best friend."

"What did you think of her?" Holly asked.

Kerry grinned. "She wasn't a bit like I thought

she'd be," she said, thinking of Jennifer's mop of light brown curls and the freckles on her upturned nose.

"I know what you mean," Holly replied with a crooked smile. "I was expecting long fangs and blood drooling out the side of her mouth."

Kerry burst out laughing. She'd had pretty much the same thoughts herself.

They spent the rest of the morning working in the stables; but as Kerry groomed Magician's gleaming black coat, her thoughts were firmly centered on the new horse. Buccaneer's wild eyes and flaring nostrils had caught her imagination. She started to fantasize about gentling him and being the only one besides Liz who would be able to ride him. She seriously doubted that Whitney Myers would be allowed to ride a horse as highly strung as Buccaneer. Whitney's riding skills were minimal, and she only won blue ribbons because her mother had bought her Astronaut, a perfectly well-trained horse.

As Kerry dropped her brushes in the grooming box, Whitney and Jennifer returned to the barn. They were both dressed in riding breeches and high black boots. Kerry stared at them curiously. Jennifer's horse hadn't arrived yet, so who was she planning to ride?

"Where's Liz?" Whitney asked. "I want to ride the new horse, and I'm going to let Jen ride Astronaut."

"In her office," Kerry said. She couldn't help smiling. There was no way Liz would allow Whitney to ride Buccaneer, in spite of what his owner had said.

Jennifer hung around the aisle while Whitney disappeared to find Liz. "Is that your horse?" she asked

21

as Kerry fed Magician a carrot. The horse nuzzled her hand gently; and when it was all gone, he nudged her pockets, hoping for more.

"No, he belongs to Holly."

"That's Liz's daughter, right?" Jennifer asked.

Kerry nodded.

"She's the one in the wheelchair, isn't she?" Jennifer persisted. "Whitney said you were her companion. Aren't you kind of young for a job like that?"

Kerry bristled indignantly and wondered what else Whitney had told her. Whatever it was, it couldn't have been flattering. "I'm almost fourteen," she said quietly, and wished Jennifer would stop asking questions. As if on cue, Robin Lovell, another member of the riding team, entered the barn. Grateful for the distraction, Kerry introduced the two girls.

"No, Whitney, you can't ride Buccaneer, and that's final!" Liz said loudly from inside her office. "I don't care what Mr. Ballantine said. That horse is much too high-strung for you to handle, and I refuse to be responsible if you have an accident with him."

"But Mr. Ballantine *said* I could ride him," Whitney protested in a whining voice as she followed Liz out of the office. "You're being ridiculous. Buccaneer's only nervous because he's in a new place. I bet he'll be fine tomorrow."

Liz halted suddenly and put her hands firmly on Whitney's shoulders. "I know you're disappointed, but I can't risk it. He's not suitable for you, or any of the kids, to ride. I'm sorry, but that's the way it is."

Whitney scowled. "Are *you* going to ride him?"

Liz laughed. "Of course I am. Mr. Ballantine has left him in my care." She looked toward Jennifer, Robin, and Kerry. "Did you hear what I said, girls? Buccaneer's off limits to all of you, okay?"

Kerry swallowed her disappointment. She was hoping she'd be able to persuade Liz to let her ride him, even if Whitney wasn't allowed to.

Whitney looked as if she was about to argue, but instead she grabbed Jennifer's arm. "Come on, Jen, let's go to the club for a swim. We can't both ride one horse, and I don't want to hang around here all day."

Holly wheeled herself out of the tackroom as they were about to leave. "Hey, Mom, can I ride this afternoon? You said you weren't busy."

Jennifer hesitated, her eyes growing wide with astonishment as she looked at the girl in the wheelchair. "Hey, I didn't know you could *ride*," she said. "Can I stick around and watch?"

"Don't bother," Whitney snapped, tugging at her arm. "It's boring and stupid. All she does is walk around the ring on a scruffy, old pony. Come on, let's go for a swim."

Kerry could have sworn she saw a look of embarrassment shoot across Jennifer's face, but then it was gone.

Kerry quickly saddled Hobo, the small brown pony that Holly used for her therapeutic riding lessons. She knew that Holly would rather ride Magician, but Liz had forbidden it. Gentle and well-trained though he was, Magician needed a strong pair of legs around him—something that Holly didn't have.

23

Kerry stood by the pony's head while Liz and Robin Lovell got ready to help Holly into the saddle. It wasn't an easy task, lifting the handicapped girl high enough so she could get her legs over his back, and it was important that the pony stand perfectly still while they tried.

Just as they got Holly onto her feet, the pony moved, and Holly almost fell over. As Liz made a frantic grab for her daughter, Kerry saw that the pony was standing on Holly's left foot. No wonder she'd lost her balance.

"You clumsy beast," Kerry muttered, and leaned against his shoulder in the hopes of freeing Holly's foot.

"Stop!" Holly cried. "Don't move him."

"He's on your foot," Liz said, and she started to push on the stubborn animal as well.

"You don't understand!" Holly cried in desperation. "I can *feel* him."

Liz stopped pushing against the pony and stared at her daughter in astonishment. "What did you say?" she asked quietly.

"I said I can feel him," Holly repeated, smiling.

"You're only imagining it, Holly," Liz said. With a mighty shove, she dislodged the pony's hoof from her daughter's foot.

Holly started to laugh and cry at the same time. Liz put her arms around her waist and eased her gently back into the wheelchair. "Do you want to try again?" she asked.

Holly shook her head. "No, but I really could feel his hoof, Mom. Do you think I might be getting

better? The doctor said it might happen, didn't he?"

Liz smiled. "Don't get your hopes up," she said gently. "You're so eager to walk again, your mind is playing tricks on you. I'm afraid you're only remembering what it *used* to feel like." She bent down, took Holly's sneaker off, and started to press her foot. "Can you feel that?" she asked, looking up at Holly's shining eyes, still wet with tears.

She shook her head.

"Or this?" Liz pressed and poked her fingers carefully into Holly's ankle, and then up toward her knee.

"Yes . . . no. Oh, I don't know," Holly wailed. "But honestly, Mom, I felt Hobo's hoof. I *know* I did. Can we call the doctor? I want him to examine me again." She turned excitedly toward Kerry and Robin. "I'm going to walk again," she said in a determined voice. "I just know I am."

Chapter Three

"Holly, they gave you *crutches*!" Kerry exclaimed, jumping to her feet and rushing toward her friend as she wheeled herself through the door. A pair of wooden crutches were lying diagonally across Holly's lap. "That's fantastic!"

"Not for me," Holly said flatly. "They're Mom's. She sprained her ankle."

"Oh, no!" Kerry cried. "Where is she?" She leaned across the wheelchair and looked toward the driveway through the open door. Liz hobbled toward her, a pained expression on her face.

"What happened?" Kerry asked. She ran over to Liz and helped her into the house.

"Mom stole the show," Holly mumbled, her voice tight with disappointment. "The doctor spent more time with her than me."

Kerry glanced at her. She looked close to tears. "What did the doctor say about *you*?"

"Just like Mom said," Holly replied miserably. "I must have imagined it." And then she shook her head defiantly. "But I don't believe them. I *know* what I felt. I wasn't wrong."

"But . . ." Kerry started to say.

Liz interrupted her. "Kerry, I'm going to need your help."

"Oh—yes—of course," Kerry stuttered, still thinking about what Holly had said. What a disappointment. "Here, lean on me," and she carefully steered the injured woman toward the couch. "You haven't told me what happened. How did you hurt your ankle?" she asked anxiously. "It's not broken, is it?"

"No, just a bad sprain and some torn ligaments," Liz replied, wincing as she sat down.

"Mom fell off the curb in the parking lot at the clinic," Holly said in a quiet voice.

"Great move, huh?" Liz said. "I'm afraid I really will need your help, Kerry. I'll have to cancel all lessons except the beginners. But the horses still have to be fed and cared for."

"No problem," Kerry assured her cheerfully. "I can handle the chores, and I'm sure the other kids will help out."

"Mom, aren't you forgetting something?" Holly said suddenly.

Liz frowned. "I don't think so."

"The new horse."

"Oh, no," Liz groaned. "I'd completely forgotten about him." She shrugged her shoulders helplessly and sighed. "Well, he'll have to wait till I'm back on my feet, that's all."

"Isn't Whitney supposed to be riding him?" Holly protested. "Let her do all the hard work."

"Very funny, Holly," Liz said with a frown. "You saw what that horse is like. No one's going to ride him except me."

"I could ride him for you," Kerry said hesitantly.

Liz smiled and shook her head. "Thanks for the offer, Kerry, but I can't let you take the risk. My ankle will heal soon, and then I can get to work on him myself. Besides, if you had an accident with him, I'd really be up the creek! Who'd do all the barn chores for me if you ended up on crutches as well?"

Kerry decided not to push it. Maybe after the new horse settled down, Liz would change her mind. She forced Buccaneer to the back of her mind as she and Liz got busy making lists of things for her to do in the next few days.

Finally Liz staggered to her feet, then winced in pain as she put weight on her injured foot. "Have we covered everything?"

"Yes, I think so."

"Except me," Holly said quietly.

"What do you mean?" Liz asked.

"Who's going to help me with these if Kerry's going to be at the stables all day?" She held up a sheet of paper.

"What?" Liz said, and then she shook her head. "Oh, Holly, can't those exercises wait a few days?"

"No, they can't," Holly replied, meeting her mother's eyes.

"Honey," Liz said patiently. "I don't want you to get your hopes up and then be disappointed if you don't

29

get results. The exercises don't guarantee anything."

"What exercises?" Kerry asked.

Holly silently handed her the sheet of paper. It was covered with diagrams and written instructions.

"Holly picked it up at the clinic," Liz said wearily. "She's convinced herself they're going to help her walk again."

"Will they?"

"Maybe—maybe not," Liz said with a hint of a smile. "But you know Holly. A cross between a mule and an elephant—stubborn, with a long memory."

Holly couldn't help laughing. "Stop teasing me, Mom. I'm serious about this. I want Kerry to help me exercise my legs in the pool. Like in the pictures. The doctor said it wouldn't hurt to try."

"I know, but he didn't promise it would help, either."

Holly stuck her bottom lip out and stared defiantly at both of them.

"I'll help you," Kerry volunteered without hesitation. And then she started to wonder how she was going to find the time to get everything done.

"Poor Kerry," Liz observed with a smile. "All of a sudden, everyone needs her."

Kerry was in the barn by seven the next morning, still half asleep. Liz had promised to come over at nine to give the beginners' lesson. Kerry had bumped into her in the kitchen, wobbling around unsteadily and cursing the crutches as she tried to make a pot of coffee.

No one else was there, and Kerry got busy, feed-

30

ing the horses and cleaning out their stalls. It took much longer doing it by herself. By the time she was half way through, she wished someone else would come and help her out. The beginners' lesson was supposed to start at nine-thirty. She'd never be ready for them at this rate.

Magician whinnied at her every time she went past his stall, but her pockets were empty. She'd forgotten his carrots. She stopped and stroked his nose through the bars, wishing she could dump everything and take him out for a nice, long trail ride.

The barn's new arrival was nervously pacing about in his stall next to Magician, and every time Kerry went by him, he flicked his ears back and forth and eyed her warily. He was still tense and upset, and Kerry wondered if she'd really be able to make friends with him.

Liz arrived two minutes before the group of beginner kids, and in no time at all the barn was in an uproar.

"But *I* want to ride Pumpkin," one voice protested loudly.

"You can't," replied another, even louder. "You rode him last time. It's my turn. Hey, Liz, tell Marcia I'm going to ride Pumpkin."

Bit by bit, Kerry sorted out the details of which kid got what horse, and then she herded the straggly crowd of riders on their ponies into the indoor arena. She carried a folding chair with her for Liz to sit on while she conducted the lesson.

Kerry left Liz with the kids and went back into the stable area. She still had to finish cleaning the stalls

31

and sweep the aisle. As she went past Buccaneer's stall, she stopped. The big bay horse turned around and stared at her, but this time he didn't put his ears back. Instead, he pushed his nose between the stall bars, as if he were looking for someone to pet him.

"You're gorgeous," Kerry whispered as she stroked his soft, velvety muzzle. Then, without hesitating, she opened his stall door and went inside. If she was going to make friends with this horse, she'd better get started right now.

"It's okay, boy, I won't hurt you," Kerry said as she quietly approached him. Then, forgetting that she had no carrots with her, she fumbled around in her pockets. He saw what she was doing and whinnied eagerly.

"Sorry, boy, but all I've got are some old M and M's," Kerry said apologetically as she looked at the few pieces of candy she'd pulled out of her pocket.

Buccaneer nuzzled her hand, hesitated a second or two, and then gobbled up the M&M's in a flash!

Kerry stared at him in amazement. "You crazy horse! You're not supposed to like candy."

Buccaneer put his nose in the air and curled his upper lip out. Then he pushed her hand gently, obviously looking for more. Kerry gave him the last of the candy, then gently and carefully started to run her hands down his firmly muscled neck and shoulders. Buccaneer seemed to like the attention, and when she scratched a ticklish spot by his withers, he curled his lip up in appreciation.

"Good grief! What are you doing in there, Kerry?" Liz leaned against the open doorway and stared at

Kerry, a look of complete astonishment on her face. "It looks like you've got him eating out of your hand."

"You could say that," Kerry said with a grin. She decided to risk asking again if she could ride Buccaneer. "He likes me, Liz," she said earnestly. "Please let me start riding him for you. I promise I won't get hurt."

Liz hesitated a moment, then her face relaxed into a smile. "Okay, you win, but if he starts to act up, I want you off his back immediately. Understood?"

"He'll be fine," Kerry said. "Can I ride him now?"

"I've got a bit of paperwork to do," Liz replied as the beginning riders crowded back into the barn. "But after we get the ponies settled, we'll work him in the indoor ring."

Kerry helped the kids unsaddle and brush off their ponies, then she ran back to the house. Holly came into the kitchen just as she was standing on a kitchen chair, searching through the cupboards.

"What are you looking for?"

"M and M's."

"Why? You got a 'candy attack' all of a sudden?"

"It's not for me, it's for Buccaneer. He's got a sweet tooth." Kerry opened another cupboard and peered inside.

Holly laughed. "I think there's some stuff left over from last Halloween, but I bet it's pretty yucky by now. It's in the cupboard over the stove."

Kerry found the candy and jumped off the chair.

"I'm coming with you," Holly said. "I've got to see this."

Five minutes later they were in Buccaneer's stall,

33

and the horse was eagerly gobbling up the candy.

"See, I told you," Kerry said.

"He'll be your slave forever," Holly warned as Kerry put his saddle and bridle on. "Just so long as he knows what you've got in your pocket!"

Kerry led the horse into the indoor arena, followed by Holly and Liz. She couldn't help smiling to herself as she thought about what an odd group they were—a girl in a wheelchair, a woman on crutches, and a horse that liked M&M's!

Liz and Holly settled themselves in the middle of the ring.

"Go ahead, Kerry," Liz said. "You can get on him now. Just walk him around on a loose rein, and then some slow trotting. Okay?"

Kerry put her foot in the stirrup and swung herself gently over Buccaneer's back. "Easy, fella," she said as she settled herself into the saddle. Then she quietly picked up her reins and squeezed him gently with her legs. Buccaneer hesitated a moment, then relaxed. He moved forward into a steady, flat-footed walk.

It didn't take Kerry long to find out that whoever had trained Buccaneer had done an excellent job. He responded immediately to the slightest pressure from her legs. When she asked him to flex his neck and accept the bit, he didn't resist.

"Try cantering him," Liz called out.

Buccaneer gracefully swung into a collected canter, even before Kerry had time to give him the proper signals. She grinned happily. The horse was voice-trained as well, and he'd understood Kerry's commands perfectly. But Liz had been right about one thing. He was super-sensitive and needed careful handling. Kerry found that out, much to her embarrassment, when she inadvertently squeezed him too hard. He broke into a fast canter, heading straight toward one of the jumps.

"Pull him away!" Liz yelled. But it was too late.

With an enormous leap, Buccaneer flew over the four-foot parallel bars, clearing them with no effort at all.

"Sorry," Kerry apologized when she pulled him into the middle of the ring. "That was my fault. I didn't have time to turn him."

"No harm done," Liz said. "At least now we know he can jump."

"Can I jump him again, maybe over the practice course?"

"Not yet. I want you to school him quietly first. Lots of big circles, and get him to bend. I don't want to rush him."

Kerry nodded, picked up her reins, and steered Buccaneer toward the rail. She was really enjoying herself. The horse was great fun to ride, and much more of a challenge than Magician. She hoped Liz would allow her to start jumping him soon. It had felt really great when they'd taken the parallel bars by mistake. She couldn't wait to try again.

Just then the phone rang, and a few seconds later Robin Lovell stuck her head around the door. "Hey, Liz, the farrier's on the phone. He wants to talk to you."

"Drat," Liz said, and hitched her crutches up

underneath her arms. "I'd better talk to him. I've been trying to reach him for three days." She turned to look at Kerry, riding Buccaneer in a wide circle at the far end of the ring. "Can you manage him all right? I've got to take a phone call. I'll be back in a minute."

Kerry waved, and Liz limped across the ring and disappeared into the stables.

Holly sat quietly in her chair and stared at the horse and rider. She couldn't help feeling a touch of envy as she watched Kerry expertly riding Buccaneer around the ring. It made her all the more determined to go on with her exercises. She was so deep in thought that she didn't notice the girl standing directly behind her.

Chapter Four

"Liz says I'm to ride him now." Whitney's voice came from behind Holly's wheelchair.

Holly jumped and turned around. "What did you say?"

Whitney ignored her. "Bring him over here!" she yelled at Kerry. "Liz told me to take over."

Kerry frowned and gently eased Buccaneer down to a walk. Then she turned him toward the center of the ring and stopped in front of Whitney. "I don't believe you," she said quietly. She was sure Liz wouldn't let Whitney ride the horse, especially if she wasn't in the ring to supervise.

"Just get off," Whitney snapped. "I saw Liz in her office, and she told me to ride him. Now, get off."

"Kerry, don't listen to her," Holly said in a firm voice. "She's lying."

"Shut up, you little creep," Whitney snarled. Then she grabbed Buccaneer's reins, jerking on his mouth.

He snatched his head away and flattened his ears back against his head.

"I'd rather wait till Liz gets back," Kerry said quickly, not making a move to dismount. She patted Buccaneer's neck. He didn't seem to like Whitney at all: His ears were still flattened back, and he had started to stamp his feet.

Whitney scowled and then turned around. Jennifer McKenna was walking across the ring toward them. "Jen, didn't Liz tell me I could ride Buccaneer? Kerry says I'm lying."

Jennifer looked puzzled for a second, then she shrugged. "Yeah, I guess so."

"I bet," Holly muttered sarcastically under her breath.

"If you don't get off that horse, I'll tell my mother," Whitney said to Kerry in a fierce whisper. "She'll be furious with you when I tell her you wouldn't let me ride."

Kerry hesitated, and then she slowly dismounted. She hated herself for giving in, but there was no sign of Liz, and she knew how forceful Mrs. Myers could be. And maybe Liz *had* told Whitney she could ride the horse. After all, that was the original plan. Perhaps Liz had changed her mind since Buccaneer had just performed so well.

"Be gentle with him," she warned as Whitney put her foot in the stirrup. "He's very sensitive."

"I know how to ride," Whitney snapped.

"Don't say I didn't warn you." Kerry stood back as the girl clumsily swung her leg over the horse's back and came down hard in the saddle—too hard.

Buccaneer snorted loudly and took off at a fast trot, with his rider frantically trying to gather up the reins and get her feet into the flyaway stirrups.

"I bet she's only doing this to impress Jennifer," Holly muttered. "Look at her! You'd think she'd never ridden before."

Kerry felt sick as she watched Whitney trying to gain control over Buccaneer. She was pulling too hard on his mouth, and Buccaneer looked as if he was about to buck her off. Then, all of a sudden, Whitney kicked him hard, and he broke into a gallop. He careened madly around the corner, almost scraping his rider off against the rails.

"Stop her!" Holly said urgently, and tugged at Kerry's arm. "Mom will have a fit if she sees this."

"How?" Kerry asked. "Throw myself in front of him?"

"Don't be stupid. Try calling Buccaneer."

"Too late," Kerry muttered as she turned around. "Here's Liz."

"Whitney!" Liz yelled angrily as she hobbled across the ring. "What on earth do you think you're doing?"

Whitney tugged at the reins and tried to turn the horse into the center of the ring. "You told me I—" Her last words were cut off as the horse skidded to a stop, sending a shower of tanbark out behind his hooves. His rider had jerked once too many times on his sensitive mouth, and he'd had enough. With a loud squeal he reared up in the air, then plunged forward, throwing his body into a violent buck. Whitney's riding hat flew off, and she was thrown forward around his neck. Buccaneer got the bit

between his teeth and took off in a mad gallop around the ring, completely out of control.

"Stop him, Whitney!" Liz shouted. She started to move toward the horse, but one of her crutches caught in a lump of tanbark. She fell over and let out a yell as her injured ankle twisted awkwardly beneath her.

"Mom," Holly cried, "are you all right?"

"Don't ask," Liz muttered grimly as she staggered to her feet. She looked around for the runaway horse. "Ease back on the reins," she called out. "No, don't yank his mouth like that!"

Buccaneer took care of the problem by himself. He thundered down the center of the ring and gave one final, gigantic buck. Whitney went flying over his head, narrowly missing his flashing hooves as she landed on the ground. The horse careened off to the far end of the ring, swerved away from the rails at the last minute, and skidded to a stop, his sides heaving with exertion. Then he laid back his ears and, with his head snaking along the ground, trotted toward his unseated rider.

"He's going to attack her!" Jennifer cried. "Whitney, get up! Run!"

"I'll get him," Kerry said, reaching into her pocket as she ran toward the loose horse.

"Watch out for him, Kerry!" Liz yelled after her urgently. "He's gone crazy!"

"She'll be okay, Mom," Holly said. "Just watch."

Her hand stretched out in front of her, Kerry caught up with the angry horse just before he reached the fallen girl. He raised his head and looked at Kerry cautiously. Then, all of a sudden, he whinnied softly and pricked his ears forward.

"Here you are, boy," Kerry said softly. She fed him a handful of M&M's and gently took hold of his trailing reins. Buccaneer nuzzled her hand for more, and she laughed and patted his neck.

"Good grief!" Liz said in astonishment. "He's like a split personality. I wonder what made him do that?"

"M and M's," Holly said with a grin.

"You're kidding!"

"Uh-uh. He's got a sweet tooth. Kerry found out earlier that he'll do anything for a handful of candy."

Liz let out a long sigh. "Well, thank goodness she stopped him. A few more seconds and Whitney would have been mincemeat!" Then her expression changed, and her mouth settled into a firm line. She limped over toward Whitney and glared down at her.

The girl's face was as white as a sheet, and she was sitting on the ground where she'd fallen, her arms hunched miserably around her knees.

"Don't you ever disobey me again," Liz said in an icy voice. "You could have been killed!"

"But . . . but you told me I could ride him," Whitney protested feebly.

"No, I didn't," Liz said slowly, barely able to control her anger. "I told you to wait till I was off the phone, and then I said I'd talk to you about it. You deliberately ignored what I said. And because of your stupid behavior, Buccaneer will be even more difficult for Kerry to manage."

Whitney staggered to her feet and angrily brushed the tanbark off her riding breeches. Her long hair had come loose from its elastic, and stray pieces hung over her eyes.

"You can forget about riding Buccaneer," Liz continued. "It's obvious you're not capable of handling him. From now on he's off-limits to you. Do you understand?"

Whitney shook her hair away from her face. "I don't care about that stupid horse," she said viciously, "or your precious Kerry. She's welcome to him."

Jennifer ran up with Whitney's riding hat and linked her arm through Whitney's.

"Come on, Whitney," she said gently, and led her friend toward the gate. Kerry, leading Buccaneer, passed close by as they left the ring. Whitney stopped and grabbed her arm.

"I'll get you for this, Kerry Logan," she said spitefully. "It's all *your* fault. You're nothing but trouble, and you don't even belong here."

Kerry tore herself loose from Whitney's grip and kept on walking. Buccaneer started to tremble, and he kept his ears back until Whitney and Jennifer disappeared from view. "Take it easy, fella," Kerry said as calmly as she could, but inside she was shaking with rage. A threat from Whitney Myers was something to be taken seriously, and she wondered what the angry girl would try next.

"You can put him in his stall now," Liz said as she pushed Holly's wheelchair toward the gate. "I think he's cooled off enough."

"Poor Kerry," Holly said softly. "Whitney's never going to forgive her for this."

* * *

44

A loud thunderstorm woke Kerry very early the next morning. She tried to go back to sleep, but the noise of the rain beating on the roof was too loud. She yawned and got up, dressing quietly so she wouldn't wake Liz and Holly.

She reached the stables just before seven, and just as she was finishing the morning feed, the phone rang.

"Hello," she said breathlessly, wondering who on earth would be calling so early.

"Is this Timber Ridge?" a man's voice asked.

"Yes. Timber Ridge *Stables*," Kerry said, just to make sure she identified herself properly.

"Good," said the voice. "I'm calling from Meadow Park. We can't get there with Miss McKenna's horse for another two weeks. Would you please tell her?"

Kerry knew that Liz was expecting Jennifer's horse any day now. "Why can't you bring it?"

"We've got a virus in the barn, and the vet won't let any horses leave till the quarantine period is over."

"Oh," Kerry answered, somewhat alarmed. "Is it bad? I mean, Jennifer's horse isn't sick, is it?"

"Tell her not to worry, Miss," the man said. "We've got it under control, and all the animals have been vaccinated. The barn manager will call her house later on and explain everything to her. Just don't forget to tell her we won't be bringing it up today as planned. Okay?"

As soon as she put the phone down, Kerry wrote a note to Liz about Jennifer's horse and tacked it to the notice board, next to the lesson schedule. She counted five kids in the beginners' class. She made a list of the names, along with the horses and ponies they would be riding. Five was all they could handle this morning because two of the ponies were still out in the paddock, muddy and soaking wet.

Then she checked the saddles and bridles to make sure they were all in good order and that no straps were broken or missing. Liz arrived just as she was finishing. "Are you sure we have enough ponies for the kids?" she asked as she limped to her office.

Kerry nodded. "Yes, I checked the list twice."

"Good. I'd hate to see what would happen around here if we didn't," Liz said with a grin. "It'd be pandemonium!"

Slowly the children started to arrive, eagerly looking forward to their riding lesson. Kerry counted them . . . one, two, three. Then two more arrived together. Good, that was the lot.

Just as she went into Pumpkin's stall with his saddle and bridle, two more children ran into the barn.

"Am I late?" a small red-haired girl asked breathlessly.

"For what?" Kerry asked.

"My riding lesson!"

Kerry groaned and rapidly counted the bobbing heads that were milling around the aisle. She frowned and shook her head. Maybe she'd counted someone twice, so she tried again. It kept coming up to seven, and there were only five horses available.

"Wait a minute!" she yelled above the noise of chattering voices. She ran into Liz's office and looked at the list of names again. There were only five.

"Help," she said to Liz.

46

"What's wrong?"

"Seven kids and five horses," Kerry moaned. "Now what do I do?"

Liz frowned at Kerry. "Didn't you write down all their names as they called in for their lessons?"

"Yes," Kerry said, and she pointed to the chart. "I wrote them in the minute I got them, like you told me to."

"You must have forgotten two," Liz said in a grim voice as she checked the chart herself.

"I'll go and fetch the other two ponies," Kerry said, wondering how long it would take her to clean them up. When she'd checked them out, first thing that morning, they were both covered with mud from head to tail.

"Don't bother," Liz said. "There isn't time. I'll sort it out, but don't let this happen again, okay?"

"Sorry," Kerry muttered, realizing that she'd never seen Liz upset with her before. But with the way her foot must be hurting her, Kerry knew Liz wasn't her normal cheerful self.

Liz solved the problem by splitting the kids into two groups. But by doing so she had to spend two hours instead of the usual one, sitting in the indoor arena. And there were more lessons scheduled for the afternoon as well.

Liz wore a pained expression on her face and was limping worse than ever when she emerged from the riding arena, just over two hours later. Kerry felt bad for her and apologized again for messing up the scheduling.

"It's okay," Liz said grudgingly. "No harm done, but

please try to be careful, Kerry. It's such a mess when there aren't enough horses, and then I get complaints from irate parents."

Kerry decided to double-check the afternoon list before she went back to the house for lunch. As she was checking the large sheet of paper closely, she thought she could see two more names in the column for the morning session. She rubbed her eyes and peered even closer. Yes, it was faint, but definitely there. Names she remembered writing in herself only two days before, in pencil.

And someone had erased them!

Kerry sat back in her chair and stared at the wall. Could Liz have erased them by mistake? No, of course not. That didn't make any sense. She thought hard for a few minutes, and idly wondered if one of the younger kids had played a stupid prank.

She shook her head slowly. No, that wasn't it either. Only someone who wanted to get her in trouble could have done something like this. And she had a sneaking suspicion she already knew who that someone was.

Chapter Five

It was well after five that afternoon before Kerry had a chance to work with Holly on her exercises. Although the rain had let up earlier in the day, the air was still damp and cool. Kerry stared at the list in her hand and then frowned at Holly, who was waiting patiently in the pool. "Are you sure you want to do this now?" she asked.

"Positive," Holly replied.

"Well, let me know if you start to get chilled." Kerry sighed and read the first item aloud: "Slowly try to move the foot from side to side."

Holly, who was hanging from the side of the pool by her arms, concentrated on her left foot.

"Well?" Kerry asked after a few moments.

Holly shook her head. "The water's moving, but my foot isn't. Let me try again." Kerry watched as Holly's foot floated motionless. "What's the next exercise?" Holly asked.

49

"Slowly try to raise the leg in the water," Kerry read aloud.

Holly tried with identical results.

"I have an idea," Kerry said, putting the list down and getting into the water. "Let me try to move your leg first, then maybe your leg will get the idea and do it on its own."

"Maybe," Holly said with a bitterness Kerry had never heard from her before. "And maybe it never will."

Kerry began to tread water to keep from shivering. "That doesn't sound like you," she said. "I can't believe you'd give up after just two exercises."

"It's not two exercises," Holly said, her voice trembling. "It's been two years!" With a start, she pushed off from the side of the pool and swam furiously toward the other end. Kerry watched as she swam until she was near exhaustion. When at last Holly pulled herself to the side, her voice was calm. "I want to go in now," she said.

"You know," Kerry began hesitantly as she helped her friend out of the pool, "you never told me about the accident."

Holly tensed up immediately, a remote expression settling over her face. "I don't want to talk about it." With an abrupt motion she pushed Kerry's hands away from her and flopped down on the grass, shivering with cold.

Kerry handed her a towel. "Please tell me," she said patiently. "It might help if you could talk about it."

Tears suddenly sprang to the corners of Holly's deep blue eyes. She rubbed at them angrily and

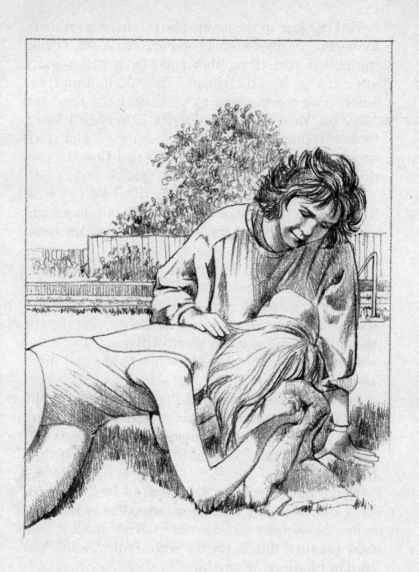

buried her face in the towel. The two friends sat there for a while, Holly silently crying into her towel. Finally she pulled herself together and began. "Dad and I were driving into the village," she said in a muffled voice. "We were going to pick up some feed for Magician. We'd stopped at a traffic light when I heard brakes scream—and a loud—crashing. . ." Her voice trailed off, interrupted by the tears that flowed freely down her face.

"Oh, Holly." Tears of sympathy filled Kerry's eyes, too. She put her arms around her friend's shoulders and held her tightly. "You don't have to say any more if it's too painful."

"I never told this to anyone. Mom's the only one who knows the whole story. But I want to tell you, Kerry." She shivered and pulled the towel around her shoulders. "I was thrown clear of the car, and the last thing I remember was a sheet of flame . . ."

Kerry gasped. So that's how her father had died. In a fire! How awful!

"I tried to get to him, but I couldn't move," Holly continued in a faraway voice. "I could see him still in the car, but then the flames . . ." She paused and caught her breath. "I couldn't save him." The girl began to sob.

Kerry tightened her hold around Holly's shoulders and, with her free hand, wiped away her own tears. "No wonder you don't like talking about it," she said gently. "But it wasn't your fault, Holly. You couldn't have done anything."

"I know." Holly had calmed down and now reached out and took Kerry's hand. "Now I've got you as upset as I am. I'm sorry."

Kerry shook her head. "You know, since I came to live with you and Liz—it's been the first time I've felt like I've had a real family since my mother died. I think I want you to walk and ride again almost as much as you do."

"I'll see what I can do about it," Holly promised as Kerry helped her into the wheelchair. They started back toward the house. "Wait a minute," Holly said before they went in. "Mom said there was a problem at the stables this morning. What happened?"

Kerry told her about the mix-up over the lessons. "I know I wrote those names in, but someone erased them." She purposely didn't tell Holly that she suspected Whitney of doing it.

"You're sure you weren't seeing things?" Holly asked.

"Uh-uh."

Holly frowned and pursed her lips. "Hey, you don't suppose Mom could have erased them by mistake, do you? She's been a bit flaky since her accident."

Kerry shook her head. "No, I've already thought of that."

All of a sudden Holly's eyes flashed angrily. "I bet I know who it was!"

The look on her face told Kerry that they were thinking exactly the same thing: The only person mean enough to pull a stupid trick like that was Whitney Myers. "But Whitney wasn't even in the barn this morning," Kerry said without much conviction.

"So what? She could have done it yesterday afternoon. I bet it was her. You know how mad she is about not being allowed to ride Buccaneer."

Kerry miserably agreed with her. She wished Whitney lived far, far away. Like Alaska, or the South Pole!

"Are you going to tell Mom?"

"No, it won't do any good," Kerry muttered. "I can't prove anything. Besides, she's feeling bad enough as it is, and I know her foot's hurting her like crazy. I guess I'll just have to watch out, that's all."

"Good luck!" Holly said as they went into the house.

Kerry had just changed out of her swimsuit when the phone rang, and a few minutes later Liz called out from the kitchen. "Kerry, why didn't you tell me Jennifer McKenna's horse wasn't coming in for another two weeks? Her mother just called and told me that someone had left a message at the barn this morning. She was just checking to make sure I'd gotten it."

Kerry went into the kitchen, puzzled. "Sorry, Liz, I forgot to tell you, but I did leave a note for you."

"Where?"

"On the wall, next to the lesson chart."

"I didn't see it," Liz said with a frown. "And I couldn't have missed it, because I was looking for something else this afternoon that I'd tacked up myself. The only note up there besides the lessons chart was one to remind me to order more hay."

Kerry's face fell. "I guess the note dropped off," she said lamely. "I'm sorry."

"Luckily, it doesn't really matter," Liz said a little sharply, "except that I felt like a complete idiot when Mrs. McKenna called. She must think I'm very disorganized."

Kerry walked slowly back into the family room, her face red with embarrassment.

"More trouble?" Holly asked.

Kerry nodded. "Yeah, I forgot to tell your mom about Jennifer's horse. I left her a note, though. I tacked it to the notice board, but she says it's not there."

After Holly had gone to bed, Kerry felt restless. She couldn't stop thinking about the missing note, so she ran over to the stables to check for herself.

The bright red push pin that she'd used to tack it up was still there, but there was no sign of the note. Just a tiny piece of torn paper remained, still hanging onto the pin. Someone had ripped the note off, leaving the pin in place.

Whitney again! Kerry thought to herself angrily.

As she returned to the house she decided not to share her suspicions with Holly. Holly had a hot temper, and Kerry couldn't trust her not to go off the deep end the next time they saw Whitney.

The best thing for her to do was tell a little white lie and admit to finding the note somewhere on Liz's desk. She'd tell Holly it had fallen off the notice board.

Two days later, right after the beginners' morning lesson, Liz told Kerry not to put Pumpkin back in his stall. His eight-year-old rider had just departed, and Kerry was about to take his saddle and bridle off.

"Why?" she asked as she loosened the pony's girth.

"I want Jennifer McKenna to ride him," Liz told her. "She'll be here in a minute."

"Jennifer's going to ride *Pumpkin?*" Kerry asked in astonishment. "She's much too big. Her feet will touch the ground."

Liz laughed. "I know, but I only want to see how well she can ride, and Pumpkin's already saddled up. It'll only be for ten minutes or so, and he's strong enough to carry her."

Kerry looked at the small pony, shrugged her shoulders, and tightened up his girth again.

Whitney Myers, followed by Jennifer McKenna, arrived in the barn a few minutes later. "Liz, you're not going to make her ride the pony, are you?" Whitney protested when she saw Kerry holding Pumpkin's reins.

"Yes, I am," Liz said firmly. "Okay, Jennifer. Come on. Let's see what you can do."

"But that's stupid," Whitney said scornfully. "She's supposed to be riding Magician, not a dumb pony."

Kerry looked at Liz in surprise. No one had told her that Jennifer was going to ride Magician, and she couldn't help feeling jealous. No one else had been allowed to ride Holly's horse except her . . . until now.

Kerry had to admit that even though Jennifer was much too tall for the pony, she didn't really look that bad on him. It was the way she rode. And when she put him into a collected trot, and got him to accept the bit and flex his neck, Kerry was quite impressed.

"She's pretty good, isn't she?" she said in a low voice to Liz, hoping that Whitney wouldn't overhear her.

Liz nodded. "Okay, Jennifer. You can canter now."

Pumpkin broke into a slow, controlled canter, picking up the correct lead right away. Kerry gasped. Pumpkin looked like a different pony, and all of a sudden he was no longer the silly fat, chestnut pony that all the kids loved to ride. He looked just like a miniature dressage horse with his head held proudly and his neck arched.

"I *told* you she could ride," Whitney said in a know-it-all voice as Jennifer cantered around them in perfect circles.

"Okay, Jennifer, that's enough!" Liz called out. She was smiling, obviously impressed by the way the new girl rode. "You've convinced me. You're free to use Magician until your own horse gets here."

Whitney shot an "I-told-you-so" look at Kerry and followed her friend out of the arena.

"That girl's had some excellent dressage training," Liz observed as she and Kerry walked along after them. "If she does as well with Magician as she did with Pumpkin, I'll put her on the riding team."

Kerry's heart fell to the bottom of her stomach. What would that do to *her*? She didn't want to ask. Maybe Holly was wrong when she'd said that Liz wouldn't dump her. After all, the riding team was supposed to be for the residents of Timber Ridge, and Kerry hardly qualified. As Whitney so often reminded her, she was just an employee. It was time to accept the fact that her riding for the team had been a one-shot affair—something that had happened only because Liz had been in a jam.

Miserably, she let herself into Buccaneer's stall and shared a packet of M&M's with him. She could hear

Jennifer and Whitney talking to Liz in excited voices as they discussed Jennifer's riding performance and made plans for the upcoming horse show.

"I'm going home for lunch now," Liz said a few minutes later. She stopped outside Buccaneer's stall, her arms loaded with books.

"What are those?" Kerry asked.

Liz glanced down at her arms. "The stable account books," she said with a scowl. "I'm taking them back to the house."

Kerry wondered how Liz was going to manage the books *and* her crutches. "Do you want me to bring them over for you?" she volunteered.

Liz smiled. "Would you? That'd be great, and then I can get them all straightened out before the auditors come."

Kerry gave her a questioning look.

"The Homeowners' Association is having their annual meeting soon, and Mrs. Myers wants all the stable books up to date," Liz informed her. "And right after that the auditors take over, so I have to have them in perfect order."

Liz bent down awkwardly and put the books on the tack trunk outside Buccaneer's stall. "I've left you the three big ones," she said. "I can manage the rest. And don't forget them, *please*," she added before walking away.

Kerry only half heard her. She was still thinking about Jennifer McKenna's incredible performance on the pony. She was really worried about her own position. She wondered if she'd be able to keep her place on the riding team; there was another horse show coming up soon, and she wanted to be a part of it. Miserably, she buried her head in Buccaneer's mane and wished she really did live at Timber Ridge like everyone else, instead of being just the "hired help," as Whitney called her.

A few minutes later Jennifer stuck her head around Buccaneer's door. "Liz told me to ask you for help when I start riding Magician," she said.

Kerry disentangled herself from Buccaneer's mane and walked to the doorway. "Where's Whitney?" she asked suspiciously. Lately, whenever Jennifer was around, Whitney was sure to be underfoot.

"She left a few minutes ago. Say, you won't mind helping me, will you?"

Kerry hesitated. She really didn't feel like helping Jennifer McKenna take *her* place on the riding team. It wasn't fair, and she wanted to tell her to get lost.

"Kerry, are you okay? You look kind of weird." Jennifer looked at her anxiously.

"You won't need any help," she said grudgingly. "Magician's a super horse. Anyone could ride him." That wasn't exactly true, but she didn't feel like complimenting Jennifer on her riding skills.

Jennifer didn't appear to notice Kerry's reluctance to talk, because she started telling her all about her family and the stables where she'd learned to ride. "Meadow Park's much bigger than this," she said, "but I think I'm going to like it better here. Prince will, too."

Kerry's curiosity about Jennifer's horse got the better of her. "What's he like?"

Jennifer smiled wistfully. "He's kind of small—only

fifteen hands. A bright chestnut, he's got four white stockings and a blaze running down the middle of his nose. He's half Arabian."

"What's the other half?"

Jennifer grinned impishly. "Kangaroo," she said with a laugh. "No, I'm only kidding. But he's a fantastic jumper, and I tell everyone that when they ask. Actually, I've no idea what the other half is."

After Jennifer left, Kerry stood brooding. She wished Liz hadn't said she wanted to put the new girl on the riding team. Even though Jennifer had been friendly enough, Kerry couldn't help but resent her.

Angrily, she shut Buccaneer's door and bent down to pick up Liz's account books. There were only two, and she could have sworn Liz had said she was leaving three books for her to carry. She checked behind the tack trunk to see if one had fallen off, but it hadn't. Figuring that Liz had changed her mind and had taken one of the ledger books with her, Kerry picked up the two books and headed for the door.

It was still quite muddy from the rain, and Kerry had to pick her way carefully across the stable yard. She was so deep in thought about Jennifer and the possibility of not being a part of the riding team anymore, that she almost missed it. Her foot touched something hard, and it moved slightly.

With a cry of horror, Kerry bent down to look closer. It was one of Liz's ledger books, soaking wet and smeared with mud. Kerry adjusted her load onto one arm and carefully lifted the cover. She gasped with dismay when she saw that several of the pages were torn. Poor Liz, she'd have even more work to do, copying them over.

Kerry carefully added the book to the pile in her arms and headed toward the house, wondering how Liz could have dropped it without noticing.

Liz and Holly were eating lunch when Kerry came through the back door. Liz smiled at her, but her look changed to alarm when she saw the muddy ledger book.

"Kerry, you didn't *drop* it, did you?" Liz asked in disbelief. She got to her feet and took the damaged book off the top of the pile.

Kerry knew in a flash that Liz hadn't dropped the book. Someone else had, and on purpose! Kerry felt trapped. She knew Liz would never believe another "I-didn't-do-it" story. She figured a simple accident was more believable.

"Gee, Liz, I'm sorry," she mumbled, thinking that all she'd done for the past few days was apologize. "I tripped, and I couldn't save it. Look, I know some of the pages are torn, but I could try and mend them for you. Or else I'll copy everything over. My writing's pretty neat."

Liz groaned as she carefully examined the damaged pages. Finally she looked up, glaring at Kerry. "I know this was an accident, but I can't help it. I'm really angry with you. I thought you were more responsible than this, Kerry."

"Mom, let her help you," Holly said, putting her hand gently on her mother's arm.

Liz shook her away. "No, I'll do it myself." And she got up and carried the books out of the kitchen.

"You're a rotten liar," Holly said quietly. "You didn't

drop that book, did you?"

Kerry shook her head miserably. Holly could see right through her. "Liz said she left three books outside Buccaneer's stall, but when I went to pick them up, there were only two. I figured she'd taken one with her, but she hadn't."

"*Someone's* trying to make Mom mad at you," Holly said slowly. "Where were you after Mom left the books outside Buccaneer's stall?"

"Inside . . . with him."

"Could Whitney have sneaked up and taken one of them without you noticing?" Holly asked.

Kerry nodded. She'd been so busy feeling sorry for herself, the barn could have fallen down around her ears and she wouldn't have noticed.

"That does it, then," Holly said. "Whitney knew Mom would blame you, and she's counting on the fact that you'll keep your mouth shut." She paused and stared at Kerry. "Is there anything else you haven't told me about?"

Kerry admitted the truth about the missing note to Liz, telling her about the change in plans for Jennifer's horse.

"Hah! So Princess Whitney *is* doing everything she can to force you out of Timber Ridge."

"She's doing a pretty good job, too. Your mom looks as if she's ready to fire me."

Holly reached out and touched Kerry's arm. "Don't say that," she said gently. "You know Mom would never do that. She really likes you, and right now she couldn't manage without you."

"Sure," Kerry replied sarcastically. "All I seem to

do is mess things up for her. Big help I am."

"So, are you going to tell her the truth?"

"No, I told you I don't want to," Kerry said urgently. "Besides, I can't prove it's Whitney who's behind all this. You know she'll deny everything."

"You're probably right," Holly agreed. "Has Mom told you about the Homeowners' Association's annual meeting? It's coming up pretty soon."

"Yes."

"They'll be voting to renew her contract then."

"And that's why I can't say anything," Kerry said grimly. "If your mother knew it was Whitney's fault that all these things keep happening, she'd be so mad, she'd go straight to Mrs. Myers and raise the roof!"

"And then she could kiss her job good-by," Holly finished for her.

"You got it. And I don't want that on my conscience, so let's keep quiet. Okay?"

"I guess you're right," Holly agreed reluctantly. "But I hate to see Whitney getting away with this. I wish there was something we could do."

"Well, there isn't," Kerry said. She tried to smile. "Let's talk about something else."

"Mom said Jennifer's a terrific rider," Holly said cheerfully as Kerry helped herself to a sandwich and a handful of potato chips.

Kerry almost choked. Talking about Jennifer McKenna was almost as bad as worrying about what Whitney was going to do next. "Yeah, she's okay," she admitted through a mouthful of crumbs.

"Hey, come on," Holly protested. "Mom said Pumpkin looked like a Grand Prix dressage horse when she rode him. I wish I'd seen them."

"Did she tell you she wants Jennifer on the riding team?"Kerry blurted out.

Holly looked startled. "No," she said slowly, "Mom didn't tell me that. No wonder you're so shook up. Poor Kerry. It's been a rotten day, hasn't it?"

"Yeah," Kerry agreed slowly, and she knew it could only get worse. With Whitney Myers on the war-path, anything could happen!

Chapter Six

Kerry tried to keep her mind off what had been happening by working as hard as she could. It wasn't easy, trying to watch out for Whitney and keep up with all she had to do. So when Liz finally agreed that Buccaneer was ready for Kerry to take him out on the trails, she couldn't wait.

That afternoon she rode off toward the woods and open fields that surrounded Timber Ridge. She'd ridden the trails on Magician several times, so she knew her way around quite well. As she passed one of the cross-country course markers, she wished Liz hadn't forbidden her to ride Buccaneer on it. He was a terrific jumper, and Kerry knew he was ready for the challenging cross-country course. But Liz had insisted that he needed more schooling over the easier hunt course in the meadow beside the stables.

Suddenly Kerry heard hoofbeats behind her, and she tensed up, thinking it might be Whitney. She'd noticed that Astronaut's stall was empty when she left the barn. Since there was no sign of them in any of the riding rings, she figured Whitney had done the same thing she had—gone trail riding.

She looked over her shoulder and heaved a sigh of relief. It was Robin Lovell on her chestnut gelding, Tally Ho.

"Hi," Robin called out cheerfully. "Want some company?"

"Sure," Kerry agreed readily. In the past few weeks of helping out around the barn, she'd gotten to know Robin quite well and was grateful for all the help the girl had given her. Without her pitching in and cleaning stalls, Kerry would never have time for trail riding. She smiled as the red-haired girl rode up alongside her.

They rode side by side when the narrow trail allowed, and Kerry felt the tensions of the past week slowly ebbing away. It was easy to forget about Whitney Myers on such a gorgeous day. The bright sunlight cast long shadows on the trail beneath her, and overhead birds were twittering and chirping merrily, sending a chorus of song echoing through the woods.

"Do you want to try the practice jumps in the meadow?" Robin asked.

"You mean the small ones near the cross-country course?"

Robin turned her head briefly. "Yes. Do you think Buccaneer can handle them?"

"Sure," Kerry replied. She knew Liz wouldn't mind if she took Buccaneer over that course. It was kid's stuff.

The woods ended, and the meadow opened up before them. It was an enormous flat field, bordered on three sides by rustic fencing. The fourth side was a low, thick hedge that separated the field from the woods. Scattered around the perimeter were small rustic jumps that the cross-country riders used for warming up their horses.

"I'm going to take the jumps first," Robin called out over her shoulder, and she cantered off on Tally Ho toward the start of the small course.

Kerry trotted into the middle of the meadow and stopped. She sat on her horse and relaxed, enjoying Robin's expert performance over the jumps. Tally Ho was a steady, solid jumper, and he and Robin had been part of the riding team for two seasons now.

"Your turn," Robin said a little breathlessly when she rode back toward Kerry. "Good boy," she added fondly, rubbing Tally Ho's neck.

Buccaneer's ears pricked up as Kerry headed toward the first jump. It was a small cross-rails, and he cleared it easily. Calmly she adjusted his stride, and he sailed over the next two fences in the same way.

"He looks great," Robin yelled out.

Kerry smiled to herself and concentrated on the next fence, a three-foot brush jump with a small ditch in front of it. "Easy, boy," she whispered to her horse and leaned forward into his neck. He gathered himself up, and they flew over with plenty of room to spare.

"Kerry, that looked terrific," Robin said enthusiastically when the pair had finished. She had gotten off her horse and was sitting on the ground as he grazed contentedly beside her. "It's amazing what you've done with him since he first got here. After what happened to Whitney, I didn't hold much hope for you."

"It's the M and M's," Kerry said with a silly grin.

Robin laughed. She knew about Buccaneer's strange taste in food. In fact, the whole barn knew about it, and the horse was well on the way to major tooth decay!

Kerry was savoring Robin's compliment when an unwelcome sight emerged from the woods. It was Whitney, and she was riding straight toward them.

Robin noticed her immediately, and her expression changed. "Hey, Kerry, there's something I think I ought to tell you," she said in a grim voice. Whitney's sudden appearance had just reminded her.

"What?"

"You're not going to like it," Robin muttered as Whitney and Astronaut drew closer. "But yesterday I overheard Whitney telling Jennifer McKenna all about what happened at the Hampshire Classic."

"You mean she actually *told* Jennifer what she tried to do to me? Like getting her little sister to wave her windbreaker just as I was going over that awful jump, and then breaking off the course markers so I'd get lost?"

"Not exactly," Robin said with a frown. "The way she told it, *you* were the one who was trying to louse things up. Not her." She paused and glanced at Whitney again. "And she also told Jennifer that Liz was going to take you off the team. According to

69

Whitney, you don't belong here."

Kerry gasped, and a cold fury settled over her like a black cloud. After all that Whitney had done to her, this was the last straw. She choked back the angry words that were welling up inside her, knowing it was useless to lose her temper.

"That horse is a vicious killer," Whitney said scornfully as she rode up to them.

"What are *you* doing here?" Robin asked in an annoyed voice. She stood up, brushing stray pieces of grass from her jeans.

"Fell off, huh?" Whitney stared at Robin with a contemptuous expression on her face.

"No, but I can see *you* did," Robin retorted.

Whitney blushed and hastily put her hands on her thigh as if to cover the telltale brown smudge on her white breeches. She'd obviously taken a tumble off Astronaut somewhere on the trail. Kerry hoped she had a few bruises to go along with the stain on her pants. It would serve her right!

"Let's get out of here," Kerry muttered as Robin tightened Tally Ho's girth. "I don't like the company."

Whitney's eyes narrowed. "I bet that vicious horse goes completely crazy out here," she taunted. "Has he tried to kill you yet?"

"I guess you got here too late to see how well he went," Robin said. "Come on, Kerry. Let's go."

"No, wait a minute." Kerry's blood was starting to boil. In spite of her determination not to let Whitney's goading get to her, she could feel her temper rising. She took a deep breath. "I'll match Buccaneer against your horse any day."

Whitney smiled. This was just what she'd been hoping for—a direct challenge that she was sure to win. "What's wrong with right now?"

"Out *here*?" Kerry replied in surprise.

"You're crazy," Robin interrupted quickly.

"I'll race you on the cross-country course. And *beat* you," Whitney declared, ignoring Robin's protest. "What's the matter, Kerry? Scared of being beaten . . . again?"

"You know racing's against the rules," Robin said, desperately trying to break the deadlock.

"Hah! Who cares about stupid old rules." Whitney snorted. She stared at Kerry. "Well, are we going to race or not?"

"Ignore her," Robin said, urging her horse forward until he was alongside Buccaneer. She reached out and grabbed Kerry's arm. "Let's get on with our ride."

Kerry shook her hand away. "You're on," she said defiantly, looking Whitney straight in the eye.

"Don't do it," Robin implored, but she knew it was already too late. The gauntlet had been thrown down, and the duel was about to begin. Robin could see it in both girls' eyes.

"We'll start from over there," Whitney said, pointing toward the far end of the meadow where two small flags marked one of the cross-country jumps.

Kerry nodded curtly, her face looking grim. She gathered up her reins and pushed her hard hat down firmly on her head. Whitney wasn't wearing a hat. Whether it was yet another way she could flaunt the stable's rules or from sheer vanity, Kerry didn't know.

"I'm ready," she said coldly.

Buccaneer sensed something was up. All the way toward the first fence he danced and skittered sideways, and Kerry knew she was going to have the ride of her life. Her anger toward Whitney had pushed all of her common sense aside, but she didn't care. All she could think of was Whitney's horrible tricks that had gotten her into trouble, and what Robin had just told her a few minutes ago.

As she approached the start of the course she knew she was letting herself in for trouble. But she couldn't help it. More than anything, she wanted to race Whitney Myers—and *beat* her.

"Now we'll see who's the best rider," Whitney said nastily when they were finally ready, standing side by side.

And then they were off. Immediately Whitney forged into the lead, pushing past Kerry as they headed toward the first jump. Buccaneer almost stumbled as Astronaut's hindquarters banged into him. But Kerry had anticipated a move like that and managed to steady her horse so that he would not fall.

"Easy, boy," she whispered into his mane as they flew over the low rustic poles between the wooden fence posts. Ahead of her she could see Whitney hunched over her horse's neck, her long dark hair flying free as the wind whipped past her. The pace that Whitney set was fast—much too fast for the difficult course ahead of them—and Kerry started to regret her impulsive decision. What if Buccaneer fell and injured himself? Liz would kill her, to say nothing of his piratelike owner.

Whitney disappeared around a bend in the track, and Kerry's heart sank. The next jump was one of the worst. Called a Tiger's Trap, it was a set of enormous horizontal logs, with just enough space between them so that both horse and rider could see what was on the other side—a dark, ominous-looking ditch filled with stagnant water. Kerry felt herself tensing up as the jump got closer.

"One, two, three . . . and up," Kerry counted swiftly to herself. She relaxed her hold on the reins and Buccaneer lifted himself up. They cleared the fence by only inches, and Kerry let out a sigh of relief. The worst was over. Or was it?

As she galloped along the wide dirt trail beside the narrow river, she suddenly realized that she'd no idea how her horse felt about water. She stared ahead of her between Buccaneer's ears and tried to remember if there was a way around the next obstacle in the course.

Tiny red marker flags flashed by her as she picked up speed. And then she saw Whitney, about a hundred yards ahead. She was shouting at her horse, urging him through the small stream that veered off at right angles to the river, forming jump number three in the course. And there was no way around it.

Astronaut was refusing the water, but Whitney raked at his sides with her spurs and lashed out across his rump with her crop. He lurched forward, splashed into the shallow water, and scrambled up the steep bank on the other side.

As Kerry cautiously approached the water holding Buccaneer in check, Whitney turned around. "You'll never catch us now!" she yelled triumphantly. Her horse reared slightly, then crashed off down the other side of the hill and disappeared from view.

Buccaneer hesitated when he saw the stream. "It's okay, boy. It won't hurt you." Kerry struggled to keep her voice and hands calm as the big horse shied away from the alien water in front of him. Gently she squeezed with her legs and urged him forward with her voice. Finally he gave in and entered the shallow stream. "Good boy," Kerry whispered, and patted his neck. There was no sign of Whitney and Astronaut, and she almost gave up. But stubbornness and a high level of anger kept her going. She recklessly plunged down into the woods at a much faster pace than she should have.

As she was approaching the next fence, a downhill log jump with a frightening drop-off on the other side, she saw her opponent. Astronaut had stopped in front of the fence, and Whitney was whipping him furiously. She turned around as Kerry approached.

"Get on, you lazy horse!" she screamed, and dug her spurs into his sides. Astronaut leapt upward and took the jump from a standstill, almost unseating his rider. They were only twenty yards ahead when Kerry cleared the fence comfortably.

Just as the cross-country course took a sharp turn back into the woods, Whitney suddenly swerved off to the right, away from the course and toward the open field that bordered the paddocks behind the stables. Kerry followed close behind. As Buccaneer

stables. Kerry followed close behind. As Buccaneer increased his speed, she could see that they were gaining on Whitney, and fast.

For a brief moment both girls galloped together, side by side. Easing herself even more out of the saddle, Kerry squeezed with her legs, and Buccaneer surged forward, taking the lead. An immense feeling of satisfaction shot through her, and she knew she was going to win.

She *had* to win! She realized with a shock that if Whitney did beat her, she'd tell everyone, including Liz. And Kerry would be in more hot water. The only way Kerry could keep Liz from finding out about the race was if she won it. Whitney wouldn't say a word if that happened.

There was only one more obstacle that separated her from victory—the stone wall that divided the field from the one closest to the stables. It was old, and in bad need of repair, but not very high. As Kerry lengthened the distance between herself and Whitney, she glanced back over her shoulder. Whitney was a good fifty yards behind her, and it was obvious that Astronaut was tiring fast.

"We just have to jump that wall. It doesn't look very high," Kerry muttered to herself as the stone wall drew closer. She squinted into the sun directly ahead of her and saw something glistening on top of the wall. With a jolt of panic she realized it was barbed wire, stretched taut and high between the old wooden posts that were unevenly spaced along the crumbling wall.

In a split second she made her decision. With all

the force she had left in her tired body, she pulled Buccaneer's head around to the left and swerved away from the deadly obstacle.

"Whitney . . . barbed wire!" she shouted, but her words were lost in the wind. Her opponent either didn't hear, or else chose not to, because she galloped past. With a mighty crack of her riding crop across Astronaut's hindquarters, Whitney rode him over the wall like a steeplechase jockey.

Kerry's thumping heart lodged itself somewhere between her chin and mouth as she watched, too stunned to believe her eyes. She was so caught up in her concern for Astronaut and the deadly wire that she forgot all about their ridiculous challenge ride. Nothing was worth risking a horse's life for. And certainly not the victory gained by jumping a barbed-wire fence.

Feeling dumbfounded, and slowly realizing that she'd lost the race, Kerry started heading back toward the woods where she knew there was a break in the wall that she could scramble through.

"Hah, beat you, Kerry Logan," Whitney's scornful voice floated across from the other side of the wall. She had ridden back to show off. Her horse was breathing heavily, and his coat was drenched in sweat. "You and that dumb horse are too chicken to take a *real* fence. It takes guts to jump something like this." She laughed triumphantly, waving her hand toward the stone wall.

Kerry didn't answer. Her eyes met Whitney's in a brief moment of mutual hatred, and then she looked away. Misery engulfed her. Not because she'd lost the race, but because she'd allowed her temper to get the better of her and had taken an unforgivable risk with a very valuable horse.

Whitney galloped off, and Kerry began the trek back to the barn. Her anxiety level rose as she got closer to the stables. She knew that Whitney wouldn't waste a minute in telling everyone how she'd beaten Kerry Logan on the cross-country course. And when Liz found out about it, as she surely would, Kerry knew she'd be absolutely furious. She had distinctly told her not to push Buccaneer too fast, and most especially to stay off the cross-country course.

She wished she could stay out in the peace and quiet of the fields with him forever, but she knew she couldn't. She had to go back and face a sneering Whitney, and what was worse, a very angry Liz Chapman.

Chapter Seven

"Kerry, are you in there? I want to talk to you!" The kitchen door banged shut, and Liz's voice sounded angry.

Kerry's heart almost stopped beating. She knew that Liz had finally heard about the race. There'd been no sign of her when she'd returned to the barn—only Whitney, who was boasting to Jennifer about how she'd raced Kerry and beaten her.

"What's the matter?" Holly looked at Kerry anxiously. "Not *more* trouble?"

Liz limped into the family room before Kerry had a chance to explain. She hadn't told Holly anything about the race; she was feeling much too embarrassed about it.

"I want you to tell me that Whitney's making it all up," Liz said, her eyes flashing angrily.

Kerry gulped and felt herself blushing.

Liz sighed loudly and sat down. "So it's true then.

I was hoping it was one of Whitney's lies, but I can see from your face it wasn't."

"Mom, what are you talking about?" Holly interrupted.

"Kerry and Whitney had a race on the cross-country course this afternoon," Liz said, glaring at Kerry. "Kerry was riding Buccaneer, and I'd told her not to ride him over the cross-country course. But she ignored me, and according to Whitney, they raced flat out, all the way."

"Who won?"

Kerry cringed. Trust Holly to say something really dumb.

"That's hardly the point," Liz snapped. "What does matter is that Buccaneer is now lame. His tendon is all swollen up, and I've called the vet."

"Oh, no!" Kerry buried her face in her hands and bit her lip hard. She didn't want to make things worse by crying.

"Kerry, *why*?" Liz asked. "And on Buccaneer, of all horses." She paused, waiting for an explanation.

"I'm sorry," Kerry blurted out. "It was dumb and stupid, and I didn't think."

"But why did you do it?" Liz insisted. "You know how I feel about reckless riding."

Kerry didn't know what to say. If she told Liz the truth about Whitney and her sneaky tricks, Liz would have a fit. She'd probably say awful things to Mrs. Myers, and then the Homeowners' Association would cancel her contract. No, she had to keep quiet and say nothing at all. Mrs. Myers would be sure to cause trouble if her precious daughter was accused of

81

making trouble at the stables.

"Kerry, I'm waiting."

She didn't answer. Instead, she looked desperately at Holly and shook her head. Holly would understand why she had to keep her mouth shut.

"I'm afraid you've left me no choice," Liz said. "I'm going to ground you. From now on, you're barred from the stables, and—"

"But Mom, that's not fair!" Holly exploded. "If it wasn't for Kerry's help, you'd be sunk. Look how much she's done for you since your accident."

Liz stared thoughtfully at Holly's defiant face. "I know," she said wearily. "And don't think I'm enjoying this, Holly. But this isn't the first time Kerry's messed things up."

"But she's only a kid!" Holly cried.

"I know, but I can't take the risk of anything else going wrong," Liz replied. She turned to face Kerry. "I'm sorry, Kerry, but I just don't know if I can trust you anymore."

Liz's words cut through her like a knife, and Kerry felt tears springing to the corners of her eyes. Hastily she wiped them away. "I guess I'd better go back to Aunt Molly's," she said miserably.

Liz stood up. "No, you don't have to do that. I'd like you to stay on and help Holly, but you can't come to the stables anymore, that's all." She turned and went into the kitchen.

"Don't leave," Holly implored. "Mom'll get over this in a few days, I know she will. Besides, who else can ride Buccaneer?"

"He's lame," Kerry reminded her miserably.

"Yeah, but as soon as his leg is better, you'll be back in the stables and riding him. Look, I know Mom. She never stays angry for long. Trust me."

Holly was wrong. Liz's anger toward Kerry changed into a polite coolness, and at the end of two weeks, Kerry knew she'd never be allowed in the stables again. And what was worse, she wasn't even needed. Liz's ankle was better, and since Buccaneer's leg had cleared up, she was riding him herself.

One afternoon, while Holly was swimming in the pool, Kerry walked over to the back fence and stared wistfully at the stables. From where she stood she could see Liz and Buccaneer in the outside riding ring. As the big bay horse soared effortlessly over the jumps, Kerry wished she could turn the clock back and undo all the awful things that had happened.

Without thinking, she pulled a packet of M&M's out of her pocket and started eating them. They only reminded of her how much she missed Buccaneer. Was he still getting his fair share of candy, she wondered, or was she the only one who remembered? She wished there was some way she could see him again. But there wasn't, unless . . .

She stopped chewing and thought hard. Maybe she *could* see Buccaneer if she was sneaky. It was a risk, but she didn't care. Her longing was making her desperate. All she had to do was wait for the right time.

It came the next day when Liz took Holly to the clinic for her checkup. As soon as the car pulled out of the driveway, Kerry grabbed the rest of the M&M's

and ran over to the stables, making sure that none of the other kids were around.

Quietly and carefully she let herself inside and heaved a sigh of relief. The only people there were a couple of maintenance men who were fixing the roof. One of them waved to her from his precarious perch on the peak of the roof as she went inside the barn.

Buccaneer whinnied happily when Kerry opened his stall door. "Hi, fella," she said quietly. "I just had to come see you. I've missed you."

The big bay horse nuzzled her hands gently. "It's okay, I haven't forgotten," Kerry told him, and she gave him a handful of candy. He gobbled it up and nudged her pocket, hoping for more.

Kerry wound her arms around his neck and hugged him hard. His wonderful horsy smell tickled her nose, and for a moment she forgot about feeling sorry for herself. All she could think about was being with Buccaneer and feeling his strong body as she leaned against him. She ran her hands lovingly down his neck and shoulder and ruffled her fingers through his silky mane.

She decided to groom him. Liz and Holly would be gone all afternoon, and she had plenty of time. On her way to the tackroom she noticed a new horse in the stall next to Astronaut. That must be Jennifer's horse, she thought. As she looked at the pretty chestnut with the white blaze on its face, she felt pangs of jealousy. It wasn't fair. Almost all the other kids had horses of their own, and she had nothing. Not even Buccaneer anymore.

Kerry lost all track of time as she groomed Buccaneer. She brushed his mahogany-colored coat until it shone, and then she carefully removed the knots in his black mane and tail. Just as she was picking the dirt out of his hooves, she heard the barn door open. Her heart almost stopped beating. Oh, no! Someone else was coming into the barn. She'd be found out!

Kerry held her breath as the sound of footsteps drew closer, wishing there was some place for her to hide. As quietly as she could, she slipped behind Buccaneer, hoping she couldn't be seen. The footsteps came closer and then they stopped—right outside the stall!

"Miss, are you in there?" a deep voice asked.

Relief flooded through Kerry as she realized it was one of the workmen. She'd forgotten all about them. "Yes," she said, emerging from behind the horse.

The workman smiled at her, his cigarette dangling from the corner of his mouth. "Would you tell Mrs. Chapman we'll be back tomorrow to talk to her about the rest of the repair work? We're having a problem with the roof."

"Sure," Kerry said hesitantly, wondering how she was going to give Liz his message without admitting she was actually in the barn. She'd have to come up with a pretty good story to fool Liz.

The workman thanked her and left the barn. Kerry glanced at her watch and decided she'd better get going as well. It was almost four o'clock, and she wanted to get back to the house before Liz and Holly returned.

She gave Buccaneer the last of the M&M's, then fed Magician a carrot that she'd brought with her. She stroked his soft muzzle through the stall bars and felt her misery return. Maybe coming to the barn hadn't been such a great idea after all. It only reminded her of what she was missing.

She heard the crackle of flames the minute she stepped outside. A small fire was burning brightly in a pile of hay and wood shavings, its flames already licking at the side of the barn.

For a split second Kerry was too stunned to move. She stared at the fire as if hypnotized, watching it grow larger and larger. Then the realization of how it must have started hit her like a ton of bricks. The workman's cigarette! He must have thrown it away when he left and not bothered to check where it landed.

Pulling herself together, Kerry ran for the hose, praying that the water was turned on. It was. As soon as she pressed the metal nozzle, a steady stream of water gushed out. She aimed it at the flames. Clouds of steam hissed upward, but the fire went out.

"Phew," Kerry said aloud. "That was a close one." Then she noticed the crumpled cigarette package. She knew she had to get rid of the evidence. Quickly she picked it up and put it in her pocket. As she kicked dirt over the blackened embers she decided to tell Liz that the workman had walked over to the back of the house with his message. There was no way she wanted Liz to find out that she'd been at the barn today. Even if she had saved it from going up in flames!

As soon as Kerry was satisfied that she'd completely hidden the remains of the fire, she headed back to the house. She was so deep in thought, rehearsing the carefully constructed story she planned to tell Liz, that she didn't notice someone standing in the shadows.

Someone had seen her putting the fire out and had purposely stayed hidden!

Chapter Eight

The phone rang a few seconds before Liz and Holly came through the door. Kerry picked it up. It was Mrs. Myers. She sounded angry, as usual. "Is Liz there?" she demanded, her voice loud enough to be heard all the way across the room.

Kerry winced and held the receiver away from her ear. "She's coming in now, Mrs. Myers. Please hold on, and I'll get her for you." She put her hand over the phone and waited until Liz had helped Holly through the door. "Liz, it's for you. It's Mrs. Myers."

Liz frowned, dropped her purse on the kitchen table, and took the phone. "Hello. Mrs. Myers?"

"How did it go?" Kerry asked Holly, keeping an eye on Liz as she talked on the phone. "What did the doctor say?"

Holly shrugged. "Same old thing. I might walk again, and I might not. They don't know why . . ."

Liz's voice exploded suddenly, drowning out the

last part of Holly's reply. "What did you say?" She gasped into the phone. Then she fell silent and drummed her fingers on the table.

Kerry and Holly stopped talking and stared at Liz. Her face had turned deathly white, and she kept shooting angry glances toward Kerry.

"Uh-oh. More trouble," Holly muttered, and Kerry had an awful feeling that she was right. She started to feel guilty about sneaking over to the stables and wondered if somehow Mrs. Myers had found out about her secret trip to see Buccaneer. But how could she? No one was there except the workmen, and she doubted one of them would have told Mrs. Myers.

"Yes, thank you for telling me," Liz said in a clipped voice. "I'll take care of it right away." She put the phone down with a bang and turned to face Kerry. "I can hardly believe it," she said angrily. "But you've left me no choice, Kerry. I'm afraid you'll have to leave, and the sooner the better."

"What?" Holly cried. "Mom, what happened?"

"Kerry almost burned the barn down," Liz snapped, her eyes flashing dangerously. "That's what happened." She stared at Kerry closely. "It seems you disobeyed my orders and went to the barn. Am I right?"

Kerry almost choked. Someone had seen her. She nodded slowly, not trusting herself to speak.

"But what about the barn, Mom?" Holly interrupted. "It's okay, isn't it?"

"Yes, but thanks to Kerry, we almost lost it. Apparently, she went over there this afternoon while we were out and smoked a cigarette. She caused a

small fire, but caught it just in time. It's a good thing Whitney saw what you were doing, Kerry, or else I'd never have known. She was there, and she saw you putting the fire out and covering it up."

"Liz, I *hate* cigarettes!" Kerry protested loudly. "I've never smoked one in my life!"

"But you had a cigarette pack and were in the barn, weren't you?"

Kerry nodded. "Yes," she said quietly. There was no use in lying about that, but she had to make Liz understand that she wasn't the one who caused the fire. Desperately, she tried to explain about the workman and his cigarette, but her words fell on deaf ears.

"Even if you didn't cause the fire, you were strictly forbidden from entering the barn," Liz said when Kerry had finished. "You disobeyed my orders. Now I want you out of here this evening. I'm going to call your aunt Molly and tell her what's happened. Then I'll drive you down to the village."

"Mom, don't!" Holly cried, her voice sounding close to tears. "I don't want Kerry to leave."

"Stay out of this, Holly," Liz said sternly. "Kerry's done enough damage around here already, and I'm inclined to believe Whitney this time. It's been one thing after another, and I've had enough!"

Kerry couldn't help it. She burst into tears and ran out of the kitchen, banging into the couch on her way through the family room. When she reached her bedroom, she threw herself across the bed. She felt the way she did when she was falsely accused of killing Black Magic, a horse at the stables where she used to ride. Mrs. Mueller, the owner of that stable, had fired her, too. And now it was happening all over again!

Whitney had finally won! She got what she wanted, and Kerry couldn't do anything about it. Even if she told Liz all about Whitney's past attempts at sabotage, she wouldn't believe her. Not now. Not after this.

Holly knocked quietly at the door and wheeled herself inside. "I'm sorry, Kerry. I just tried to talk to Mom, but she wouldn't listen to me. She told me to stop telling tales and to come and help you pack."

Kerry sniffed loudly and sat up. She ran her hand through her tousled hair and tried to stop crying. The only thing she wanted now was to get away from Timber Ridge as quickly as possible. Even Aunt Molly's tiny apartment seemed like heaven compared to this.

In ten minutes she was packed. She dragged her knapsack into the family room just as Liz was picking up the phone. "Please don't call Aunt Molly, Liz. I'd rather tell her myself."

Liz shrugged and dropped the phone back on its hook. "Suit yourself," she said. "If you're ready, let's go."

Kerry hesitated. She didn't want Liz to drive her to her aunt's. She needed to be alone, and Liz was the last person she felt like spending time with. Even five minutes in the car would be too much! "I'll ride my bike," she muttered, and hefted the knapsack across her shoulders. It was full of the stuff she'd need right away; maybe Aunt Molly would come and get the rest of her things later.

Liz nodded curtly and disappeared into her office.

"I'll phone you tomorrow," Holly said tearfully as Kerry dragged her bike out of the garage. "Mom will have calmed down by then, and I'll tell her the truth about what's been happening. It'll be okay, I know it will."

Kerry hugged her quickly, then jumped on her bike before she started crying again. She didn't hold out much hope that Holly would be able to convince Liz of the truth. As she steered down the hill toward Winchester, she hoped Aunt Molly wouldn't ask too many questions about her sudden return.

Aunt Molly, her gray eyes shining happily, was delighted to see her. "How long can you stay, Kerry?" she asked when Kerry burst through the door.

Kerry dumped her knapsack onto the kitchen table and forced herself to smile. "I'm back for good."

"Why, dear? Don't the Chapmans want you to work for them anymore?"

Kerry shook her head. "Nope. Liz's ankle is all better, and Holly . . . Holly . . ." Her voice trailed off, and she took a deep breath. "They don't need me anymore," she finished quietly, hoping the half-truth would do the trick. She didn't feel like trying to explain everything to her aunt. It was much too complicated, and Kerry knew that anything she tried to say would come out all garbled and confused. She gave her aunt a quick hug and headed for the bedroom before the tears started again.

Holly phoned early the next morning. "It's no use, Kerry," she said mournfully. "Mom's still furious with you. She won't even listen to me. I'm sorry."

"That's okay," Kerry said quietly. She knew Holly wouldn't get anywhere with her mother. Liz's anger was real, and she'd never get over it.

"I miss you," Holly said.

"Me, too."

"I'll come and see you soon," Holly said, but Kerry knew she wouldn't. The hill from Timber Ridge down to the village was too steep for Holly's wheelchair, and Liz would never offer to drive her.

Holly promised to phone again soon, but when she'd hung up, Kerry felt lost and alone. It was as if the time she'd spent at Timber Ridge with Holly and the horses had never happened. And here she was, stuck in Aunt Molly's apartment, with no friends, and no place to go.

She looked at the calendar hanging on the wall over the phone. Her father wouldn't be home for several more months, and Kerry knew she'd go crazy from boredom before then. Miserably, she sat down on the couch and started to cry again. If only she'd told Liz the truth from the beginning instead of trying to handle things herself. It hadn't done any good, and now she was back where she started. Alone in Aunt Molly's apartment, with nothing to do except feel sorry for herself.

Holly called three days later with the news that the Homeowners' Association had voted to renew Liz's contract.

"That's great," Kerry said without much enthusiasm. Of course they'd renewed her contract. Mrs. Myers was probably delighted that Kerry was no longer living at the Chapmans' house and was rewarding Liz with the promise of a job for another year.

"Look, Mom's taking the younger kids to a horse show on Saturday. Why don't you come up and see me then?"

"Sure," Kerry replied sarcastically. "And when Whitney sees me with you, the fat will really be in the fire."

"We don't have to go to the stables," Holly replied. "She won't know you're here if we stay inside the house."

"I know," Kerry said. She missed Holly dreadfully, but she knew that going to the house and not visiting the barn would make her feel even worse. It would only remind her of all the good times she'd lost.

"I'll call you on Saturday. I know we can work something out," Holly promised before she hung up.

Kerry sighed and sat down in front of her dressing table. Her horse show ribbon, the one she'd helped the riding team win on Magician at the Hampshire Classic, was draped over the corner of her mirror. It cut into her reflection and made a red, white, and blue fringe above her green eyes. She stared at the ribbon and remembered how happy she'd been when she'd won it. It felt like a million years ago.

She tore her eyes away from the painful reminder and gazed at her reflection in the mirror. Her face looked pale and white, framed with a shock of dark brown hair that was sticking up in defiant little tufts.

Kerry scowled at herself and picked up her brush. Aunt Molly would certainly notice something was wrong if she went around looking like a mess. Then she'd start asking questions like "Why don't you find something to do?" or "Maybe you ought to go and visit Holly today?"

As she dragged the brush through her untidy hair, Kerry wondered what the horses were doing. Was Buccaneer missing her? Was anyone else feeding him M&M's? And even worse, had Liz changed her mind and allowed Whitney to ride him yet?

An enormous wave of anger and jealousy flared through her. She tried not to think about heavy-handed Whitney riding a sensitive horse like Buccaneer. Surely Liz wouldn't do that. Or would she? Kerry wasn't sure about anything anymore.

Chapter Nine

Two hours after Liz and the younger kids left for the horse show on Saturday, Holly wheeled herself over to the barn. Even before she reached the stables, she could hear Whitney's radio playing at full blast. It was coming from the small, three-stall barn in the far corner by the paddock fence.

For a moment Holly was puzzled. Then she remembered her mother telling her that they'd moved three of the horses out of their usual stalls while some repair work was being done on the main barn. She wheeled herself over to the small barn.

"Hey, Whitney, are you in there?" Holly yelled loudly above the noise of the radio. Buccaneer stuck his head out of the stall on the left and whinnied at her. "Whitney!" Holly shouted even louder.

Whitney leaned over the stall door with Astronaut's head beside her. She scowled when she saw Holly. "What do you want?"

Then Jennifer McKenna's head appeared over the middle stall door. "Hi, Holly," she said with a smile.

"Turn your radio off, Whitney!" Holly yelled, trying to make herself heard above the noise. "I want to talk to you."

Whitney disappeared, and the music ended abruptly.

"Does Mom know you've brought your radio back to the barn?" Holly asked, remembering the frayed cord and broken plug.

"It's been fixed," Whitney snapped. "Any more questions?"

"Yeah. Are you going riding?" Holly crossed her fingers and hoped for the right answer.

"No, I'm grooming Astronaut for kicks!" Whitney sneered, waving a dandy brush at her. "Of course I'm going riding."

Holly gritted her teeth, keeping herself from losing her temper. As sweetly as she could, she asked, "How long will you be gone, Whitney?"

Whitney shrugged. "A couple of hours, I guess. Why? You going to have a wild party while we're gone?" She paused, an unpleasant grin spreading over her face. "I know what you're up to. You're going to invite Kerry up here, aren't you?"

Holly felt her face turning red; anger boiled up inside her. "It's all your fault, Whitney. If it wasn't for your lies, Kerry would still be here. It was *you* who ruined Mom's ledger book, wasn't it?"

"You can't prove it," Whitney replied scornfully as she opened the stall door and led Astronaut outside. "Anyway, I'm glad Kerry's gone. She didn't belong here."

"And it was you who spread the rumor about her smoking in the barn," Holly continued angrily. "You saw what happened, and you know it wasn't her."

"Of course it was Kerry who started that fire," Whitney said as she swung herself over Astronaut's back. "She was always sneaking around, smoking cigarettes in the barn."

Holly choked back her anger. It wouldn't do any good to keep Whitney at the barn with a stupid argument. She wanted her gone—as soon as possible.

Jennifer and Prince emerged from the middle stall. "Let's go, Whitney. I want you to show me the cross-country course."

Whitney laughed as she picked up her reins. "Yeah, I'll show you how I beat Kerry Logan!"

As soon as the two horses were out of sight, Holly took herself back to the main barn and into her mother's office, where she immediately picked up the phone. "Hi, Kerry. It's me. The coast is clear. Mom's at the show, and Whitney's just gone trail riding. Meet me in the barn as soon as you can."

"I'm on my way," Kerry replied.

"Hurry up. Whitney and Jennifer will be back in a couple of hours." Moments after she'd hung up, Holly wheeled herself into Magician's stall. He whinnied happily when he saw her, not in the least afraid of her wheelchair.

"You'll see Kerry soon," she promised him as she stroked his nose. He nuzzled her hand gently, and Holly laughed. "Here you are, you greedy horse!" She reached in her pocket and fed him a carrot.

Suddenly Magician tensed up, and his ears flicked

back and forth. He trembled and started pacing around his stall. Holly wheeled herself out of his way, wondering what had upset him. He neighed once, loudly, and sweat broke out across his shoulders.

"What's wrong, boy?" Holly asked anxiously as she wheeled herself out of his stall. It was too dangerous for her in there if he started to act up. She shut the stall door and watched him continue to pace around his stall. He kept on putting his nose up to the window, high above his head.

Suddenly she heard another horse neighing. It was coming from the other barn. Holly relaxed and smiled. "I bet that's Buccaneer. I'll go and keep him company till Kerry arrives." She told Magician to settle down and promised to come back later with more carrots.

But as soon as she got outside, she understood the reason for Magician's restlessness. Smoke was pouring out of Astronaut's empty stall in the small barn, and Buccaneer was going crazy! No wonder Magician was so upset. He must have smelled the smoke.

Suddenly a gust of wind blew a cloud of smoke in her direction, and Holly felt herself being swept back in time. The flames and smoke pouring out of the small barn reminded her of another fire—in a car. She shook her head, trying to banish the painful memories. This wasn't her father. This was a horse, trapped inside a burning barn, and she had to save him. This time, she *had* to do something to help.

Buccaneer neighed again, instantly bringing Holly back to the present. She stared at the smoke spiraling upward. It was like watching a disaster movie, and for a split second she was too horrified to move. Then the horse kicked violently at his stall door.

"Help!" Holly screamed at the top of her voice. "Help, anyone. The barn's on fire!"

But no one answered her.

The terrified horse neighed again, and in that moment Holly knew it was up to her. She had to get Buccaneer out of his stall before he burned to death. It was only a matter of minutes before the fire would spread to his end of the barn.

With all the strength she possessed, Holly wheeled herself toward the burning building, feeling her lungs fill up with smoke as she got closer. She choked, and wondered how she was going to get Buccaneer out of his stall. From her chair there was no way she could reach the door latch.

Unless . . . !

Suddenly she knew she could do it. If she could somehow lean against the fence, she just might be able to reach the door latch. The only problem was, the fence stopped about six feet short of the stall. Her eyes smarting from the smoke, Holly wheeled herself next to the fence. She reached out and grabbed the middle rail. Then she slowly pulled herself out of her chair. She couldn't feel anything in her legs, but somehow she was standing up!

Holly gritted her teeth and, using every ounce of her strength, pulled herself toward the stall. She forced her legs to take one step at a time. The strain on her arms was almost too much from the effort of holding herself upright, but she didn't care. She had to reach Buccaneer before the flames did.

The terrified horse screamed again, his eyes rolling with fear. As the sound of his shattering kicks against the door reverberated through the air, Holly let go of the fence and lunged forward. Her hands clawed the air in front of her, and she managed to grasp hold of the top of the stall door.

Shaking violently and almost overcome by smoke, Holly pulled at the door latch. But her strength had deserted her. She couldn't move it. With a loud groan she felt her knees buckling underneath her, and she slid to the ground. She'd failed, and now she, too, was in trouble.

She started to panic. The smoke was getting thicker, and she could hardly see. "Help!" she screamed as Buccaneer's hooves bashed violently against the door.

Through a haze of smoke she heard someone yelling her name. "Holly! Holly!"

She rubbed her eyes and looked toward the main barn. Relief flooded through her as she saw Kerry running toward her.

"Help!" Holly screamed. "Get Buccaneer out."

"You're in the way!" Kerry yelled. "I've got to move you first." She grabbed Holly's arms and quickly dragged her out of the way. Then in a flash Kerry pulled the door latch free and ran to Buccaneer's stall.

Buccaneer, his eyes showing white with fear, was huddled in the far corner of his stall. "Come on, boy," Kerry coaxed urgently. The stall was rapidly filling with smoke, and she could hardly see him. The terrified horse wouldn't move. Kerry took off her windbreaker and wrapped it over his eyes. Maybe if he couldn't see the smoke, he'd let her rescue him. She grabbed his halter and dragged him outside.

"Turn him loose!" Holly yelled. "We've got to get out of here. Look!"

No sooner were the words out of her mouth than a shower of sparks flew into the air and landed all around them. Small fires sprung up where the sparks had ignited wisps of hay. Kerry grabbed Holly's wheelchair. "You'll have to help me," she said.

With Kerry's help, Holly lurched to her feet, wobbling unsteadily as she groped for her chair. Quickly Kerry got them both out of range of the erupting fire and into the main barn.

"I'm going to call for help," Kerry said as she raced into Liz's office.

"What about Buccaneer?"

"I'll catch him in a minute." Kerry dialed the emergency number and told the Fire Department what had happened. They promised to be there within five minutes.

"You wait here," she said to Holly when she hung up. "I'm going to get Buccaneer."

She ran outside, pulling a packet of M&M's out of her pocket. She had to catch Buccaneer before the Fire Department arrived; the sirens were sure to make him even more panicked than he already was. She found the horse near the front gate, covered in sweat and shaking violently. He kept on rolling his eyes, and for a few tense moments Kerry wasn't sure she'd be able to catch him.

"Come on, fella. I've got something for you," she said coaxingly as she carefully approached the terrified horse. She held out her hand. "Come on, please take them."

Buccaneer hesitated, then reached out and nibbled at the candy. Gently Kerry took hold of his halter and guided him toward the riding ring. He'd be safe there until all the fuss was over.

She found Holly sitting in her chair, watching the fire as it engulfed the small barn. Her face was deathly pale, and she was covered with smears of dirt and soot. "You look awful," Kerry said with a grin.

"So do you," Holly replied, "but thank goodness you arrived when you did. I thought it was all over. I couldn't get that door open by myself."

Kerry suddenly remembered where she'd found Holly's chair. At least ten feet away from Buccaneer's stall. She looked at Holly in astonishment. "How did you get out of your chair?"

Holly stared at her and smiled. "I guess I—I must have walked!" She gulped and then burst into tears. "I can't believe it, Kerry. I must have walked."

Kerry put her arms around her and hugged her hard. "Yes, I guess you did, Holly." She bent down and pressed against Holly's legs. "Can you feel anything?"

Holly sniffed back the last of her tears. "I think so. It's not much, but I can feel *something.*"

With its sirens going full blast, the Winchester Fire Department arrived, and in no time at all a team of men and hoses got the raging fire under control. In less than ten minutes all that was left of the small barn was a pile of blackened rubble and smoking embers.

Whitney and Jennifer galloped into the stable yard

just as Ed Fisher, the fire chief, was asking the girls if they had any idea of how the fire could have started.

Whitney jumped off Astronaut's back and pointed a finger accusingly at Kerry. "I bet it was *her*." She sneered. "She started the other fire we had."

"Wrong!" Holly cried. "Kerry wasn't even here when this one started. If it wasn't for her, we'd have lost Buccaneer."

Ed Fisher frowned and wrote something down in his notebook. "Tell your mother I'll phone her when I get the results of our tests," he said gravely. "I'm sure we'll figure it out."

Kerry left Holly arguing loudly with Whitney, and went to check on Buccaneer. The sweat was starting to dry on his coat, and he looked a mess. His mane was all tangled up, and Kerry's fingers were itching to groom him.

She fumbled around in her pocket and found a few stray M&M's. "Come on, fella. It's time you went inside." She took his halter and led him inside the main barn. His stall was full of planks of wood from the repair work, so she tied him up in the cross-ties and got busy with a stiff brush.

"Kerry, Mom's back!" Holly suddenly cried, wheeling herself into the barn. "She found out about the fire. Someone at the horse show had an emergency radio, and they heard the Fire Department calling the volunteers for help."

"Where's Whitney?" Kerry asked, sweeping the brush across Buccaneer's shoulder.

"She and Jennifer went off to jump the hunt

course," Holly replied. "Look, I need you to help me. I want to be standing up when Mom gets here."

"Kerry, what on earth are you—" Liz's angry voice rang out from the end of the barn a short while later. Kerry didn't have a chance to reply. Holly was leaning heavily against her, and she was too busy making sure they both didn't fall over to explain anything to Liz.

"Mom! Mom!" Holly shrieked as she wobbled unsteadily beside Kerry. "I've got something to show you!"

Liz's eyes opened wide with astonishment as she realized her daughter was actually standing. Supported by Kerry's arms, Holly took two faltering steps toward her. "Good grief, Holly!" Liz exclaimed. "What happened?"

"I'm walking, Mom. Look at me!" Holly shrieked happily. Then her legs folded beneath her, and she and Kerry landed in a pile of hay, laughing and crying hysterically.

Chapter Ten

Liz rushed forward and put her arms around Holly. "I can't believe it," she said, hugging Holly as hard as she could. "Was I seeing things, or were you really walking?"

Holly sat up and brushed the hay out of her hair. She reached out and grabbed Kerry's hand. "I can walk, Mom, and it's all because of the fire."

"How? What happened?" Liz asked as she hugged Holly again. "You're *really* walking? I can't believe it. It's a miracle!"

Holly grinned. "I was here alone when the fire broke out, Mom. I had to do *something*!"

Buccaneer snorted and stamped his foot. Liz stared at him and raised her eyebrows. "What's he doing in the cross-ties?"

"His stall's still full of wood," Kerry said quietly. "Where shall I put him?"

"Use Pumpkin's stall. You can turn the pony loose

in the paddock for the night," Liz replied. "Oh, and thanks, Kerry," she added as Kerry led the chestnut pony out of his stall toward the barn door. Then she turned her attention back to her daughter. "I think you'd better tell me what's been going on, Holly. And why is Kerry here?"

Holly took a deep breath. "I asked Kerry to come and see me while you were out, Mom. I missed her so much, and . . . and . . ." Holly broke off and shook her head. "Nothing that happened was her fault, Mom. I tried to tell you, but you wouldn't listen."

"But—"

"Mom, let me finish. When I got to the small barn, Whitney and Jennifer were about to go trail riding. And after they left, I saw smoke coming out of the empty stalls. I tried to open Buccaneer's door, but the latch was stuck. Kerry arrived just in time. If she hadn't . . ." Holly paused and pulled a grim face. "If Kerry hadn't turned up when she did, I'd have gone up in smoke, along with Buccaneer!"

"Thank goodness she got here," Liz said slowly. And then she looked closely at her daughter's face. "Something tells me there's more to the story."

"Mom, do you remember all the stupid things that kept happening around here? Like the mix-up over the lessons, the note you never got, and your ruined ledger book?"

Liz nodded. "What about them?"

"None of them was Kerry's fault," Holly said in a steady voice.

Liz looked at her curiously. "But Kerry said—"

"I know. She was covering up."

"For whom?"

"Whitney."

"Holly!" Liz exclaimed. "That's ridiculous. Why on earth would Kerry do that? I don't understand."

"To stop you from going off in a rage and yelling at Whitney—and Mrs. Myers."

Liz looked at her blankly. "I don't get it," she said slowly. "I think I'm missing something here."

"Kerry was afraid you'd lose your job if you told Mrs. Myers that Whitney was trying to sabotage her," Holly explained patiently. "And that's why we didn't say anything."

Liz shook her head. "I appreciate your misguided help, Holly, but don't ever do anything like this again. From now on I want you to promise that you and Kerry will tell me when things go wrong. You can't take it all on your own shoulders and try to fix it. It doesn't work."

"I know," Holly admitted ruefully. "But we didn't know what else to do. Whitney was doing everything she could to force Kerry out of Timber Ridge, and she succeeded, too."

"But I thought all that nonsense was over when Whitney got her gold medal," Liz protested.

"Oh, no." Holly shook her head emphatically. "She's furious over what happened with Buccaneer. And that's why she accused Kerry of starting the first fire." Holly's eyes grew angry. "She even tried to blame this one on Kerry, Mom. But Kerry wasn't even here when it started. She arrived just in time to save Buccaneer and me."

Liz sighed and turned around as Kerry came back

into the barn. "I feel awful about this," she said quietly to Holly. She stood up and put her arms out toward Kerry. "I'm so sorry, Kerry. Holly's just told me everything. I owe you a huge apology. Please forgive me for not believing in you."

"That's okay," Kerry said as Liz put her arms around her and gathered her up in an enormous hug.

"No, it isn't," Liz replied. "I've been awful, and I wouldn't blame you one bit if you refused to come back and live with us."

"I'd love to come back," Kerry said, blinking back tears. As she looked around the barn, a warm feeling flooded through her. It felt so good to be back where she belonged.

Early the next morning Liz took Holly to the clinic for a checkup. "You'd better watch out," Holly teased as she was getting into the car. "I'm going to take your place on the riding team!"

Kerry grinned as the car pulled out of the drive. She wouldn't mind losing her place on the team to Holly. It would be worth it, just to see her ride Magician.

All the way to the barn she thought about how great it would be to have Holly well enough to ride her horse again. But her smile faded when she stopped at Buccaneer's stall. In a few more weeks his owner would come and get him, and she wouldn't be able to ride him anymore. She wished she had a horse of her own, but that was like wishing for the moon. She didn't have any money, and good horses cost a fortune!

She opened Buccaneer's door and slipped inside.

He nuzzled her hand, and she fed him the last of the M&M's. "I'm gonna miss you," she said quietly into his silky mane.

The phone rang, and Kerry reluctantly tore herself away from the big bay horse. She ran into Liz's office and grabbed the receiver. It was Ed Fisher, the fire chief. "Please tell Liz to call me," he told Kerry. "Tell her we know what caused the fire."

"What was it?" Kerry asked.

"A radio. One of its wires must have shorted out and caused a spark. That's what caused your fire."

Kerry frowned as she hung up. What radio? Holly hadn't said anything about a radio. She puzzled over the mystery until Liz and Holly returned an hour later.

"Tell me what the doctor said," Kerry said as soon as they walked into the barn. Holly was stumbling along on her mother's old crutches, and Liz was doing her best to stop her from falling over.

Liz guided Holly into her office and helped her into the chair. Then she sat down on the tack trunk next to Kerry. "The doctor told us that what happened yesterday must have 'unlocked' Holly's mind."

Kerry blinked. "Huh?"

"Her paralysis was caused by that terrible car accident," Liz went on. "We all knew Holly wasn't permanently damaged, but her mind refused to let her walk. The shock of the car accident and her father's death had put a wall up between the part of her brain that controlled her walking mechanism and her legs."

"I always felt so guilty about not being able to help

115

my father," Holly interrupted quietly.

"Holly," Liz said. "Don't. It wasn't your fault."

"No, Mom. Let me talk. I've got to get it out in the open. I've been living with it for two years." She turned to face Kerry. "For a long time after Dad died, I had the awful feeling that I ought to have done something . . . anything. But I couldn't move. And when I thought Buccaneer was going to die, I don't know . . . I just knew I had to do something this time."

A faint smile played at the corner of her mouth. "The doctor said it's going to take lots of physical therapy and hard work, but he thinks I'll really be able to walk again one day, and it's all because of the fire."

Kerry suddenly remembered the fire chief's message. "Liz, Ed Fisher called, and he said that the fire was caused by a radio. Something about the wires shorting out and causing a spark."

"A radio?" Liz said slowly.

"Whitney!" Holly cried. "It was her fault. Oh, I don't believe it."

"Holly, what on earth are you talking about?"

"Whitney had her stupid radio in Astronaut's stall," Holly said. "I remember telling her to turn it down. She had it on full blast."

"The one with the broken plug?" Liz asked.

Holly nodded. "Yeah, but she told me it had been fixed."

"Well, I guess she lied about that, too, didn't she?" Liz stood up and frowned. "I think the time has come for me to have a quiet word with Miss Myers."

"Can I watch?" Holly asked mischievously.

"Sorry, Holly. This is something I have to do on my own, and it's long overdue!"

Liz surprised them with the news that Whitney had been grounded for two weeks.

Holly pulled a silly face. "I wish it were two years!"

"Hey, it's better than nothing," Kerry said quickly. "Liz, what happened?"

"Whitney's father was there, thank goodness, and he was furious. Mrs. Myers tried to protect Whitney, but he overruled her. She's confined to the house, and she can't come to the barn until the end of the month."

With Whitney out of the way, Kerry relaxed and spent the next week riding Buccaneer as much as she could. Since Liz's ankle was all better, Kerry wasn't needed as much in the barn, and she divided her free time between schooling Buccaneer and hanging out with Holly.

Holly's legs were getting stronger every day, and she hoped to be riding Magician again before the end of the summer. She was almost fanatical about doing her leg exercises. Holly spent so much time in the swimming pool that Kerry teased her about turning into a shriveled prune.

Kerry was riding Buccaneer on the hunt course one afternoon when Jennifer rode up on Prince. "Can I talk to you, Kerry?" she asked shyly as she pulled alongside the big bay horse.

"Sure," Kerry said, wondering what she wanted. She hadn't seen much of Jennifer around the barn

since the fire, and she figured it was because Whitney was grounded.

"I'm really sorry about what Whitney tried to do," Jennifer said. "I just found out about it, and I can't believe anyone could be so mean."

Kerry stared at her in astonishment. "But I thought . . . I thought she was your best friend."

Jennifer shook her head. "Not exactly. She was just the only person I knew at Timber Ridge." She hesitated and glanced down at her saddle. "After what I said to her, I don't think Whitney will ever speak to me again!"

Kerry raised her eyebrows in surprise. This was the last thing she expected. "What did you say?"

Jennifer shrugged. "Oh, something about cheating, and lying, and letting other people take all the blame."

"Wow!" Kerry said. "What did she say after that?"

"She said she didn't care, and that I was getting to be a drag."

Kerry burst out laughing. She'd enjoy sharing that one with Holly. Whitney had said exactly the same thing when Monica Blake moved out.

Just then she heard Holly yelling at them to come back to the barn. "Mom's got great news!" Holly shouted. "Come on, hurry up."

Kerry gathered up her reins. "I wonder what she wants," she said with a smile. With Jennifer cantering beside her, she headed back to the barn.

"Mr. Ballantine just called," Holly said as soon as Kerry jumped off Buccaneer's back.

Kerry's heart almost stopped beating. That wasn't

"great news." It was awful. It could only mean he'd be coming to get Buccaneer, and she'd never see him again.

Holly noticed her expression and smiled. "Don't worry, he's not going to take Buccaneer away yet."

"So, what did he want, then?"

"I'll let Mom explain." Holly propped her crutches under her arm and made her way back into the barn. "Come on. She's in her office."

Feeling more and more puzzled, Kerry followed behind, leading Buccaneer. She quickly took his saddle and bridle off and put him in his stall.

Liz was smiling when Kerry sat down on the tack trunk in her office. "Okay, first of all, we get to keep Buccaneer for another month or so. Kerry, so you can stop worrying."

Kerry heaved a sigh of relief. "I guess I'd better buy some more M and M's."

Liz laughed. "The great news is that Mr. Ballantine's film company wants to use Timber Ridge for a location shot in their latest film."

"Kerry, isn't that great!" Holly exclaimed. She lurched toward the tack trunk and sat down awkwardly beside Kerry. "Imagine, a movie being filmed at Timber Ridge."

While Holly fired questions at her mother, Kerry sank back against the wall and smiled to herself. The movie plans sounded like fun, but more important, Buccaneer would be staying longer than she'd thought.

Quietly she left Holly and Liz talking at the tops of their voices and went back to Buccaneer's stall. "I guess you'll be sticking around a bit longer, fella," she said fondly to the big bay horse. She slipped inside his stall and wound her arms around his neck. "I don't have to say good-by to you . . . not yet."